Compromising Arrangements

Sexy
Stories
Collection

VOLUME 40

6 EROTIC SHORT STORIES

KELLEN PRIME

Publisher's Note: This is a work of fiction. Names, characters, places, and incidents are a product of the author's imagination. Locales and public names are sometimes used for atmospheric purposes. Any resemblance to actual people, living or dead, or to businesses, companies, events, institutions, or locales is completely coincidental.

Compromisng Arrangements/ Kellen Prime. -- 1st ed.
Xplicit Press, an imprint of TLM Media LLC

ISBN-13: 978-1-62327-571-6
ISBN-10: 1-62327-571-7
eISBN: 978-1-62327-621-8

Printed in the United States of America

.

CONTENTS

1 WEEKEND AT THE LAKE

Preface

Couples have the best sex, or so they say. Apparently, this has everything to do with familiarity and comfort, the very things that many people avoid. On this weekend away, a couple finds out just how much fun it can be when you know the limitations (or lack thereof) of the person standing naked over you dripping onto your bare chest...

The water from the lake glides off her tan, falling on to Christopher's chest. Hayden and her husband need this weekend like they need oxygen. It's necessary and long overdue. The deckchair is sturdy enough to hold not only the stout, athletic Chris, but his wife also, who now straddles her man on the wooden frame perched on the raised deck of the lake house that's to be their home for the next two days. This weekend is about reconnecting, which means swimming together and fucking. They're done swimming.

Whatever disconnect Hayden had felt between them is belied by her husband's modest erection straining under his Speedo. Six inches isn't considered much, but for a man just under five foot five, it's plenty. Chris is one of those men who are proof that if size does in fact matter, it only matters in as far as you didn't know what to do with the size you're given. All the credit for their fantastic sex life went to Chris, which was part of the reason for this trip. The other part was that, for the past couple of months, they've had to share their tiny, two-bedroomed apartment with Hayden's sister and her husband – not the most ideal houseguests for a couple only a year into their marriage.

As a result, Hayden has been feeling like the problem. And in true I-know-I'm-the-cause-of-this-and-I'll-do-anything-to-fix-it fashion, she managed to get them a great deal on the lake house as only an up and coming entertainment journalist can. She had pulled every string and leverage every contact to ensure that both herself and Chris, a paralegal, had nothing to do this weekend. It's amazing what people are willing to do for tickets to an Aerosmith concert. So here they are, wet and willing on the deck of an unassuming waterfront house just outside Atlanta.

Chris's dick is a solid piece of equipment, already delivering warm rushes up and down his wife's thighs despite her bikini-covered cunt just brushing against the still-covered cock. He lies there, enjoying her efforts, knowing she isn't the world's greatest tease, but appreciating the effort anyway. She really doesn't need to do anything, because despite her insecurities, he is in absolute love with her and still finds her as sexy as when they had first met in college. He enjoys fucking her and she enjoys being fucked by him. It also helps that they're genuinely in love.

It's not long before his Speedos are on the floor, his cock positioned for penetration, his wife easing it into her pussy. She bends over to kiss him, a move that tightens her cunt enough for him to need to thrust a little to create the necessary friction. She lifts herself up and arches backwards, Chris taking her breasts in his hands as she rides him in small gentle circles. There's no rush and so he ceases to thrust as soon as thrusting becomes unnecessary.

The side of Hayden's bikini provides an interesting additional sensation for Chris's stick, almost like he was getting a hand-job and a fuck all at the same time. He likes it. He enjoys watching his beautiful wife, five feet, perfect tits, perfect ass, perfect abs, every bit the gymnast she was in college, performing on top of him. She doesn't do it often. But then again, he doesn't give her much chance to. This wasn't selfish. It's just that he really enjoys blowing her mind.

Hayden's movements are controlled, as are the muscles in her pussy. She drops her ass almost between his thighs and pushes out behind herself, taking his dick with her. Slowly to the left, then forward, lifting her ass before veering gently to the right, completing the circle in the original sitting motion between his legs. Chris's dick expands with delight, enjoying the warmth of his wife's cunt.

The joys of just being able to fuck without having to contain themselves had nearly been forgotten. But even now, all alone on an uninhabited side of the lake, there's still a measure of restraint. But Hayden is determined to rock the socks off her husband. She widens her circles, squeezing her pussy tight around his penis, varying the pressure and intensity, causing him to whimper, take loud breaths in an attempt to avoid a premature ejaculation, which was always the case when he wasn't in control. Somehow, he knew she needed to be in the driver's seat. Unfortunately, she didn't have as deep an understanding of his sexual dynamic as he did of hers, and it isn't long before Chris coats the inside of his wife's cunt with his load.

He knows she hasn't cum yet. He also registers the disappointment on her face because they both know this wasn't the event her actions had intended. If anything, she had just facilitated a rather abrupt ejaculation. She sighs, not sure what to do, needing to get off him and go off to feel sorry for herself in the shower. He pulls her down and kisses her, holding her hips firmly in place so that his cock stays put. He sways slowly from side to side, creating just enough sensation to keep his cock from going completely limp. No words are necessary as Hayden surrenders to the expert.

Chris takes her butt-cheeks in hand and parts them as he forces his own ass off the chair, effectively thrusting his now solid cock into his wife's juicy pussy. He pulls himself up to a sitting position and takes his wife's knees, locking them over his elbows. He proceeds to clasp his hands behind her back. This completely voids the possibility of a slippery exit due to his own goal. She can't move now unless he moves her. And his dick is going nowhere, not with Hayden so completely enveloping it.

The pillow on the deckchair gives his ass just enough room for him to make short stabs into her cunt. She grabs his head briefly and then wraps her arms around his neck. She takes his hair into her mouth, occasionally biting into his forehead, biting into his scalp. Her pussy is literally being tickled pink, her clit blooming as the slippery cock dances around inside, not quite in and not quite out. Chris understands a vagina in ways that only a man with the satisfaction of his partner in mind can master. He knows how to separate fact from fiction and he knows how to work with the various cunt conditions that can present themselves in the course of fucking.

Kissing her sends wave after wave of warmth down into his wife, heating her cunt even more. Her own flow now drains out of her along with his jizz, warming his cock and sack, creating the perfect condition for simultaneous orgasms. His second load isn't as filling as his first, but his overall response, the grunts, the contracting of every muscle followed by the systematic release of pleasure, are indication enough that this is one mother of an orgasm. Hayden screams, then takes Chris's tongue into her mouth and sucks hard. Enough said...

The sun beats onto their naked bodies, side by side on the chair, facing each other. Every doubt that Hayden had is now confirmed, Chris assured only of his own ability to work it. But without words, the situation seems doomed to perpetuity if this weekend doesn't yield the desired results. Hayden's thoughts drift to the book she'd been reading in secret, The Art of Satisfying Your Man, and she wonders if the most basic trick, taking control and surprising him with midday sex, has left her feeling even more inadequate. Was it a good idea to spend another precious moment of their weekend following the advice of a woman who probably had a phenomenal sex life? She wondered if it wasn't just best to resign herself to being satisfied by her man instead, never knowing what it feels like to leave him licking his fingers.

Chris's tongue finds her mouth as he fingers her clit. He looks deep into her grey eyes, telling her everything she needs to hear without saying a word. Chris's full lips are warm against Hayden's, his finger warming up as it slides into her cunt, already willing to receive him. She wants to touch him but can't bring herself to. It feels like her first time all over again and she hates that the part of her that he is enjoying right now is in fear of him. She hates that her husband so intimidates her own sexuality. She parts her legs just enough in the lying position to allow his middle finger unrestricted access.

Hayden kisses him back, trusting that he is good enough a kisser to make up for her failure even in this department. Of course, she's a great kisser, but everything else has hazed over her perception of herself. She kisses him mostly because there's no escape from her husband's mouth, just as there is no escape from the three fingers plowing her pussy. She pushes into his hand, and he pushes deeper into her cunt. She raises her leg over his body and starts to fuck his fingers, unsure where his cock is.

Her back finds the pillows, Chris now on top of her. A few more minutes of finger fucking, bringing her so close to climax she can't breathe, so kissing is aborted in pursuit of oxygen. Hayden pants, her head to the side, her eyes now on the view of the water just beyond, her mind on the fire between her legs. A gasp as Chris trusts his cock inside her, a swift deep stab. Another gasp as he pulls out his entire shaft, except for the head, then digs the whole tool right back into the pleasure-hole beneath him. Hayden's legs wrap around his, her hands now finding his ass, not spreading, but pushing him down on to her; pushing him into her.

The thrusts are intense, his cock

seeming longer for the extent to which he extracts before each plow. The walls of her pussy play with every inch of the cock, not wasting a moment as the thick tool rams into it repeatedly. Chris's breathing quickens; his pace too. There's no steadying things now because they've both crossed over into the land of no return. He fucks her harder now, almost savage as he needs his own cock to shoot its load and release the blood that has the entire length of it aching with pleasure. Deeper, harder, he thrusts into his wife until she starts to gush, her pussy pouring out the liquid that will put out the fire his dick has caused. A few more solid thrusts, sucking on her neck, breathing into her ear, and both of them explode and collapse in a satisfied heap.

The sun dances across the sky, making way for the moon and the night. The plan is to take a long shower together and then cook. It's warm enough to eat outside so that's exactly what they do. Through dinner, there is a lot of talking but just as much avoiding. Chris doesn't want to ask Hayden what the problem is, knowing in his heart what it is but avoiding the confirmation. They've been married for a year, but together for four. The sex has always been fantastic, but in all honesty, it has been one-sided. Chris was the Don Juan, and Hayden was the body that happened to be privy to his expertise. The woman in her needed to change this. But how, when Chris's ability was all the affirmation needed by the man in him?

The sun rises arrogantly over Saturday, showing off childishly as red, pink, and orange dance down from heaven onto the lake. Hayden covers her eyes as the shimmer from the silver water blinds her. The coffee in the cup on the ledge has gone cold, her thoughts having completely distracted her from the brew. Her husband lies naked in bed just inside the door and here she is, standing like an awkward schoolgirl trying to figure out how to wake him with a sexual surprise that will rock his world. She hates that she feels like she needs to prove herself, but she does. If only she could find a way to pleasure her husband and lead him to have just one of the super orgasms he gives her. It really bothers her that he never climaxes as wildly as she does.

Naturally there are the standards, wake up with your cock in my mouth, or open your eyes to the sensation of my fingers on your balls, or the even more adventurous taking of his morning glory in hand and easing it into my vagina so that he opens his eyes to the full sensation of being ridden. The list wasn't exactly endless and the options seem utterly boring. Of course, if he did any of the above things to her they would absolutely drive her insane with pleasure. This was probably because it would be him doing them to her. She couldn't imagine being touched by anyone than Chris in a sexual way, not at all. Not since that first time back in college when he had, unknown to her, put into practice all the theory he had soaked up from books, videos, and the Internet.

Again, it is Chris who takes the initiative, his "morning glory" surprising her as it brushes deliberately against her perky ass, lightly draped in fabric. He kisses the side of her face and then reaches around her for the cold coffee on the ledge. He downs it in one sip, not because he enjoys cold coffee, but as a sort of revenge for her not warning him that it wasn't exactly hot. She laughs as she imagines the look on his face, her giggle inviting a hand up her inner thigh under the tropical wrap she has on. "What's a man to do for a little warmth around here?" he asks cheekily. She smiles and parts her legs, giving in to his request for heat.

Chris uses his index and middle finger to make quick alternating taps on her thigh and then up toward her cunt, before the tapping eventually finds her clit. He plays her fleshy lips as he would a piano during the frenzied staccato of "flight of the bumble bee." She grabs onto the ledge as the sensation becomes an absolute invasion and the two fingers take advantage of the traces of moisture coming out of her. They slide into her as he takes her ear in his mouth, mouthing and then nibbling his thank you's.

Hayden absorbs the view as her husband's fingers feed into her the pleasure she knows so well. The beauty of the scene in front of her is augmented as the pleasure between her legs heightens. How he knows just how to touch her is something she decides, at least for the moment, not to ponder. She dismisses it as one of his deeper mysteries and moves on to the place where this mystery reveals itself by the complete turning out of her pussy, an event heralded by the insertion of another finger. Three of Chris's fingers inside her and she is ready to collapse. She holds tighter on to the ledge before half-turning toward her husband and holding on to him instead. He lifts her off the ground and carries her inside, his fingers not once hinting that they might leave her cunt.

In the bedroom, he pauses to lay her on

the bed. His fingers resume their fucking and her pussy responds with more moisture. He goes as deep as she seems comfortable and then wriggles around like a paranoid octopus with just three tentacles. She grabs onto his head, him kneeling between her legs so as to take in this interesting predicament her pussy finds itself in. His fingers seem right at home as time after time, they find the slit and make their way inside. She bites into his head as she usually does when he gets to the max entry of three, but this time the bite comes after a largely involuntary jolt forward.

Chris's mouth says a slippery good morning to her cunt as his tongue meets her pussy shortly after the eviction of his fingers. He tastes her such that you would think he would be writing a rather important examination regarding the many flavors of his wife. She can't help but arch her back and kick her legs. She rests her knees on his shoulders and pushes her feet toward the ground, just out of her reach. The move, though, is sufficient to ground her as her husband drinks his fill of her.

It takes just one move for Chris to lift himself off the ground and penetrate her. As he stands, her knees still on his shoulders, she falls back in such a way that her pussy meets his cock mid-air. A short downward stab and he's all the way inside her. That she is already more than sufficiently "satisfied" is evident on her face and he just takes himself home, his wife's hot pussy serving up the perfect breakfast. His load is shot quickly and the glory of the morning is effectively dealt with.

It's in the shower that Chris for the first time allows himself to really notice that there is something amiss with Hayden. He knows, as does any sensible man, not to ask and to wait for her to come to him with whatever it was.

"If there's something you want to talk about honey I'm here, whenever you're ready." This is all he needs to say to let her know that he's aware, but that he won't push her. She appreciates this and lathers his back. She enjoys touching her husband and proceeds to give him a deeply sensual massage as the warm jets of water spray over them.

Hayden doesn't give herself enough credit because in less than two minutes, Chris is lost to her touch. He melts under her fingers as she digs into the tissues of his neck and back. She works her hands, the individual strengths of each finger exploited, all the way up into his head. He closes his eyes as the suds make their way down his face. He braces himself against the side of the shower, looking up into the spray to clear his face.

His moans are louder during the massage than they are when he cums and this bothers Hayden. She dismisses this though for the moment, not wanting anything to take away from the one thing she seems able to do to Chris that gets him to "that place" she wishes she could access during fucking. She knows her husband though, and she is aware that he's always enjoyed being touched, more so outside of the context of sex. He likes talking her into rubbing his shoulders or his back, brushing his hair, or even playing with his eyebrows. He enjoys this sort of abstract affection.

Hayden works down his firm butt and onto his thighs. She massages his legs completely, getting onto her knees in order to really get in there. She can't help glancing up toward his cock to see what, if any, effect her touch is having on him. Despite his moans and groans, his circumcised cock hangs limp between his legs. She imagines snaking up between his legs and taking it into her mouth but chooses to keep doing what seems to be working for him instead.

By the time she has completed the massage, Chris looks as though he has just risen from the deepest most pleasant sleep. He knows that there is no way that the look on his face doesn't tell her everything she needs to know about the great job she's just done, and so he just kisses her and then washes her hair. They get out just as the water starts to go cold and a moment later they have breakfast in the kitchen.

Chris looks across at his wife as she fingers a stray drizzle of maple syrup from her lips. The smell of eggs and cinnamon give away their French toast breakfast. She smiles as she catches his stare, the silence comfortable, and their glances familiar. This was the way of their love. It was an unspoken familiar comfort that had taken them by total surprise at their first meeting in college. They knew in a moment that they would have a profound impact on each other's lives. In the strange familiarity of breakfast, they both remember the day...

The library was its usual graveyard, save for a few scholarship students who knew that their grades determined whether or not they stayed. Chris was studying for a mid-term and Hayden was keeping herself busy while her roommate "got busy." He noticed her through a gap in the shelves, as is often the "boy meets girl" shot in cheesy films.

There were a thousand ways for him to approach the situation, any one of them fairly acceptable for first year college students, but something about this girl with her safe brown hair and her unpretentious sweats topped off with bedroom slippers that looked like Dalmatians, made him want to get this right. He walked toward her and away from her several times, before her gestures suggested she was getting ready to leave, at which point he dropped his books on her desk, looked her in the eye and said, "help me study?!"

She did help him, and then they talked until five minutes before he had to rush off to write his exam, which he failed. She made up for distracting him by going on a date with him. This date was nothing more than an ice-cream cone on the steps of her fraternity house at midnight. Chris did that with all their subsequent dates, making them about manipulating all the things that were all college. 24-hour diners, vending machines, libraries, sports fields, swimming pools, theater stages set for Romeo and Juliet... All these things became the backdrop for what was the most original courtship Hayden had ever had.

It was a year before they even thought of sleeping together. This had nothing to do with physical attraction. Hayden was a gymnast and Chris played football and hockey. So they had the bodies that many of the other students envied or wanted in their beds. But theirs was such a mature and emotional connection that to rush any part of it would be to sabotage the beauty they had both realized early on could be theirs for a very long time.

The invitation to the mountains for a weekend hinted Hayden that Chris was ready for them to explore each other sexually. Her acceptance confirmed that she felt the same way. The cabin he had booked was perfect, a log effort with an open plan and a central fireplace. They could be on the double bed and be able to enjoy the view of embers in the hearth and the view of the forest through what was essentially the kitchen and living room window. Chris had found the place online.

He had liaised with them such that upon arrival the room was drenched in roses and fresh vanilla. A milk bath had been drawn and the fire was crackling, making the entire space toasty and inviting. They were in the room ten minutes, just enough time to orient themselves and unpack the little they had brought, before Chris did something that immediately confirmed for Hayden he was the man she would marry. He stood up and took off all his clothing, looked at her as she took in the sight, and then rather coyly said, "Well, this is me. It isn't much, but it's all yours, if you'll have it. If you'll have me..."

She stood up and walked over to him.

She stood in front of him and removed all of her own clothing, taking his hand and touching it to the places that became naked and exposed. She started to touch him only once she was totally naked herself and he explored her body with her. For the longest moment they touched, and kissed, and then touched some more. They kissed each other in the places that they admitted to each other that they had issues with, Hayden's lips kissing the tip of Chris's penis as he pointed this out to be an area of concern. His flaccid penis was still unimpressive despite almost tripling in size upon hardening. Hayden knew that this wouldn't be an issue. Chris knew this wouldn't affect what he would be able to do to her and for her.

They had crossed over the line that would have made them college fuck-buddies, when they waited a year to sleep together. And now, this new exploration, unlike any experience they had had with previous lovers, meant that if nothing else, what they would do with one another would have meaning. It did. From the first taste of his cock as she took it into her mouth all the way to how tenderly he ate her pussy. There was something so deliciously deliberate about the way he touched her that she thought he had a replica of her hidden somewhere that he had been practicing on.

He had of course been making love to her in his mind for a year. And when they eventually got together in that perfect moment, he was ready. She had seven complete orgasms over the course of that weekend. He had one. This didn't bother her, as she knew that this man had intended for the weekend to be about her. What she hadn't anticipated was that Chris would make every day of their lives since together about her...

A hot cup of coffee is the perfect end to a great morning. The day will be spent bobbing around on the lake in large rubber tubes, followed by lunch at the quaint restaurant in the village a short way up the hill. If Hayden was going to rock Chris's sexual socks, it would have to wait till tonight, or late afternoon perhaps, when they were back in the safety and privacy of the lake house. In the meantime, she would allow herself to just be in love.

The sunset was as childish as the sunrise had been. If nature could be bottled then this lake would be a prime source; the beauty of all things natural here was just exaggerated. After a brief consultation with her instruction manual – the guide she had hoped would help her reach her man sexually and surprise him – she slips it back under the heap of magazines in the bathroom and pulls the chain, just for effect. She checks herself in the mirror and undresses completely, in the hope of replicating their first fuck shortly after arrival.

She exits the bathroom naked and makes her way to the kitchen, collecting the chocolate, strawberries, honey, and whipped cream she had brought per instructions in her book. They had been carefully disguised as a part of the necessities, so the sight of them together on the table has Chris curious, as does his naked wife. He throws her a smile and then mouths the question on his mind. She doesn't answer.

Supplies ready, she undresses her husband and lays him on the sturdy table. Chris is surprised by this and it shows so much on his face, that Hayden's own face registers discomfort. Why she would be doing this if it makes her feel awkward is something he doesn't understand but he knows that there is probably something she needs to resolve within herself, so he plays along. The smell of warm honey makes him salivate and the warmth on her chest makes him wince, but only for the brief moment it takes for him to realize that the warmth is comfortable.

Hayden visibly reminds herself of

something and then rushes off to her bag, returning with a blindfold. In the dark, Chris now relies on his sense of smell to know what's going on. He also relies on the fact that he trusts his wife. This helps him to relax. The honey is drizzled in letters and shapes on every available part of his body and then slowly licked off. The touch of Hayden's tongue on his skin sends the necessary signals to his cock and he's very quickly, very hard. But the honey seems to avoid his aching dick.

A few strawberries, some chocolate and cream are fed to him. He thoroughly enjoys the taste and texture of three of his favorite indulgences. From the sound of things, Hayden feeds herself the same combination. She chews briefly, half-kissing Chris, whose mouth is also full. She hangs her pussy over his mouth and then proceeds to add her husband's cock to the bevy of delicious ingredients. The sensation completely flabbergasts him, his dick slithering around to figure out what was what. Her pussy drops onto his mouth and he proceeds to chew on the remaining delights in his mouth, nibbling punani by default.

For all her efforts though, where the instruction ends, this point where his dick is in her mouth and his mouth is on her pussy, Hayden loses the moment. With no instruction, she has no idea what to do.

She sucks on her husband a little more until she's swallowed the contents of her mouth and his mouth too is empty. The sixty-nine is suddenly nothing more than a sixty-nine. Chris senses the somewhat forced nature of the head he is getting, not sure if he should continue the indulgence or just do what he does best. To avoid the risk of embarrassing his wife by losing his erection in her mouth, something possible only because he hates that she's so uncomfortable and won't just talk to him, he slides himself down so that their mouths meet.

"Whatever did I do to deserve such a treat?" He really is sincere. Hayden cannot answer, knowing that this isn't how it should be going, knowing that again it would be him and not her that makes the rest of the experience memorable. She can't help feeling like a glorified masseuse. She can't help, in her most fragile moments, feeling like nothing more than a hot body with a cunt that can serve Chris's needs without really fulfilling them.

Chris pulls her down and kisses all her doubts and insecurities away, albeit just for the moment. But when Chris kisses her, there is nothing else that exists in the entire universe, not inside her, and not outside of her. He makes it all go away, whatever it is. He does this even when he has no idea what it us. He kisses her and gets them both on their feet in one continuous movement. He knows that despite his prowess, this is no time to downplay her efforts. He takes advantage of the urgency her efforts instilled and thrusts his dick in her cream-laced pussy, as he lifts her onto his waist. The table is just high enough for him to sit her on without losing his vantage.

He forgoes his need to wow his wife and chooses instead to play into her game. If only she knew that the mere thought of her did that already. He rests his lips on hers, his tongue in her mouth, then hers in his. His dick is bringing down the walls of her vagina and making her pussy drip more than just cream onto the wooden table. He smiles at the thought of the next group who would be here, the smile fading as he thinks of the possible escapades of the last.

There is no speaking as he loses himself in his wife. She grabs onto him. His dick digs for something in her it seems unable to find, the search bringing immeasurable pleasure to them both. Hayden enjoys this ravishing, an unfamiliar but not altogether unbearable side of her husband. A side that she almost dares assume she brought out in him. Chris continues to fuck her on the table until the piece of furniture has moved across the floor and is now stable against the wall.

Chris comes out of his semi-coma induced by the heat of Hayden's cunt and realizes that this is so far from the type of fucking he had prepared himself for all those years ago, that he doubts he will be able to cum, and after almost an hour of raw pounding his dick is sensitive and uncomfortable and he imagines the delicate tissue of his wife's cunt to be slightly bruised. He can't keep this up and withdraws, a loud sigh, the disappointment immediately registering on Hayden's face. They both know that the jig is up. He hates that he sort of lied to her. She hates that she allowed herself to believe the lies his dick was telling. In her head, though, she knew that the man fucking her absentmindedly wasn't her husband and so she allows that man to leave them.

"I'm sorry" is all he can muster.

"Don't be." She's gutted.

They shower separately and realize that this attempt "pleasing" each other has brought them apart. Chris will have none of it and Hayden knows that the last thing she needs is for the weekend to end up being the straw that broke the camel's back. Her issues would need to be addressed alone, in private, and she would have to just accept that she had a perfect husband and that despite her lacking he was a great lover.

Again, he makes the conscious choice not to ask her outright. Instead, he walks out of the bathroom and points to the fact that he still hasn't cum. His dick is limp and she fears he may be mocking her. He points out that there is nothing wrong with the sensory perception of the tool and that if she would just be so kind as to gently take the cock in her beautiful mouth and ever so gently, ever so slowly suck on it, he might ejaculate. This needs to happen without him getting hard though, the sensitivity from the earlier rouse making complete erection painful.

And so the games begin. When his dick starts to fill with blood, she moves to his balls and sucks on them, a distraction that seems to put his cock to sleep. Whatever is going on in his head, Chris has the almost supernatural ability to rewire his cock, inverting its responses to familiar sensations. Again, his flaccid dick is in his wife's mouth. The long gentle sucks continue. The dick is practically motionless in her mouth as she sucks on it as a child would a nipple. The only real feeling is now concentrated at the tip which is in the back of her mouth as her throat opens and closes with semi-swallows.

Knowing that his cock won't get fully erect now for the pressure provided by her throat he starts to thrust slowly. He enjoys the warmth of her mouth and she thoroughly enjoys the weird sensation of soft dick in her mouth. With the utmost care and patience, she manages to draw cum from his rod and his dick fully engorges only after the last drops leave the tip.

There is a moment that hangs between them that is almost uncertain. But this is not an uncertainty that makes the earlier issue as much of an issue. It is an uncertainty that makes them interested in each other. There is new curiosity, one that comes from knowing that there are things about each other's bodies that are yet to be discovered. There is suddenly so much more room to play.

Chris has managed to ensure his wife of her ability as a woman to make him climax. This happens with a flaccid dick that was just moments earlier too sensitive to cum. He had managed to somehow work past the almost excruciating pain that he actually was feeling in order for his wife to get the needed confirmation of his satisfaction that a load of semen would be. He leaves her to her own thinking and goes to run cold water over his penis for a very long while.

The rest of the evening is spent cuddling. Hayden rubs herself up against her husband like a kitty cat, purring as his warmth sends pleasure through her. He loves that even like this they are okay, no need for full-on lovemaking as confirmation of love. He holds her tight, speaking to her of everything and nothing. She listens to him, enjoying the sound of his voice, kissing some of her responses, him nibbling some of his. Their communication is intimately tactile.

The hours drift by and they fall in and out of dreamless sleep. There is a series of light petting as well, more for her, since he had an orgasm and hers was cut short. She is rewarded for her patience by a series of climaxes that wet her undies enough for her to need to clean up. She returns without replacing her underwear and her husband licks her pussy for good measure, sending her upon final climax into an incredibly satisfying sleep.

Sleep doesn't come for a while yet, and Chris takes in the vision that is his wife. He watches her sleeping and lets himself fall in love with her all over again. He plays the events of earlier back in his mind and hopes to himself that there will be no more nonsense. There is a moment that he contemplates bringing her insecurities up at breakfast the next day but he decides that provided she doesn't try another stunt to get him act a fool, everything will be fine.

The problem with her is not that she is inadequate. The problem that faces beautiful Hayden is that she doesn't know how perfect she is. If anything, there is many a time when Chris feels undeserving. But he makes the conscious decision not to entertain inadequacies, perceived or otherwise, and to focus on making the absolute best of every situation he finds himself in with his delightful wife.

Sleep is eventually too close to avoid and they are soon fast asleep. The grays of night play into the room and there is in a silence, no more of the nonsense that had plagued them in the early part of the afternoon. Peace falls over the lake house as husband and wife are locked in an embrace that makes everything else make utter perfect sense.

Sunday morning is anything but easy despite all of his best efforts. Hayden wakes up with a beautiful breakfast already laid out on the deck and the promise of even more beautiful weather. The lake is calm and there is not a cloud in the sky. It's impossible for both of them to avoid plunging into the cool water before settling down to eat. Nothing on the tray runs the risk of getting cold, the meal made up mostly of fruit and oatmeal cookies, muesli and yoghurt.

The swim is all they need to get the circulation going. They laugh and play around in the water for a long time, enjoying the cold. Hayden watches her husband disappear under the blue and surface near her, touching her. She enjoys his invisible hands feeling on her from below. The game seems better when he plays it; there is a juvenile awkwardness when she tries it. Sensing another competition, he pulls her from the water and they eat, shivering.

Hayden runs a bath for them, needing the warmth this will bring to their entire bodies. They settle into the bath and do nothing but soak up the heat and bubbles. Her eyes find the stack of magazines and the side panel of her book. She wonders if she should give it one more go, a final attempt at getting a solid explosion from him that she starts and finishes. She plants a kiss under his chin and fondles his cock, sufficiently recovered.

Disappearing under the water, she takes his dick in her mouth and gives the meat a place warmer than the bath water. He enjoys this, reminding him of their earlier days back at college, after they started fucking, when she used to play around with her athletic abilities. She would blow him under water while doing a handstand, and once she fucked him in a split until they both climaxed. She did have her moments. But these moments worked because they were spontaneous. There was a planning to this new Hayden, a forethought that just made the entire exercise futile.

She comes up every minute or so to breathe. With each decent she is greeted with a slightly harder dick. When she satisfies herself that he can get into her with no real strain, she turns to face away from him and guides him into her pussy. She rests comfortably on his lap and in the warm soapy water, rides the cock in her until her husband wraps his arms around her and holds her in place, a signal that he's cumming. She smiles to herself despite her incomplete satisfaction.

She stands above his head and allows the water to fall over his face. He finds the inside of her cunt with his fingers, something that always works her into a quick state. He gets her turned on to the point that she starts to fumble clumsily in the bath. He pulls her back down to sitting and rests himself on top of her, as his fingers continue to fuck her under the cooling water. A quick turn of the faucet reheats the water. In the new warmth, he feels up into her cunt.

It takes just moments for her to climax. Their lips meet and they recline for another half hour just enjoying where they are. The picture of Hayden rising from the water again aroused Chris and he feels the need to fuck her; more than he wants to make love to her. He wants to forget what the underlying pulses have been of the weekend and go back to that cabin in the mountains where he first exposed himself to her when their insecurities were attractive and drew the right kind of attention.

Intercepting her at the bathroom mirror, Chris traces delicate kisses down Hayden's back, then bites gently into her bum. She giggles. He kisses her all the way back up to her neck and then pulls gently with his teeth on his favorites, her ears. He cups her breasts as he watches her watching him in the mirror. His bites into her neck and shoulder make her touch herself. The sight of her own fingers running down her naval and then disappearing between her thighs solidifies his cock instantly.

She isn't inside her pussy, her fingers gliding over the entrance and digging high up her thighs. She reaches behind her for his cock and pulls it through so that the head and some of the shaft are visible. The top of Chris's dick now massages her clit as her fingers assault the dick. She teases it, guiding it toward her hole and then away. Chris reaches for his cock wanting to help with the entry but she pushes him away. They both laugh.

A moment later Chris is on his haunches, kissing the side of his wife's thigh, parting her legs so that his fingers are visible in the mirror. She watches as his middle finger is carefully inserted into her pussy. Chris and Hayden both have a fondness for fingering. The appendage disappears into the perfect pussy and then dances around inside it. The sensation is enough to send Hayden onto her tiptoes. She steadies herself on the bureau and plants her feet into the ground, a little further apart for the purpose of stability.

Chris doesn't take his eyes off his and Hayden's reflection as he parts her vagina with the fingers on one hand and gives the fingers of the other hand each a turn to explore the inside of the pussy before them. He bites into her leg as the sight of it all sends spasms and then shards of arousal through him and he needs a mini outlet for it all. With no hand to attend to his dick all he can do is sink himself into his wife, albeit it gently, with his teeth. He kisses her up as close to her pussy as possible without losing his balance and then pauses to inhale the scent of her.

His enjoyment of his wife is evident. Every finger that he withdraws from inside her is then inserted into his mouth before the next one is pushed into her again. He allows all his senses the pleasure of experiencing Hayden. She is generous with her juices as well, knowing this pleases her husband. Hayden gasps as each finger brings her closer and closer to orgasm. She screams when eventually Chris stirs the depths of her cunt with his large index finger until she coats his hand with liquid heat.

Chris licks up the juice from his hand and then gently lap up all traces of it from her pussy and its surrounds. Hayden enjoys this post-explosion cleanup just as much as she relished the pre-explosion workout. She takes a few deep breaths before pulling her husband up to meet her. She plants the most intimate kiss on his lips and then pulls his tongue into her mouth with her own. She works herself down to his cock and takes it into her mouth. She swallows it all the way to the base and then works her way slowly back up, tracing circles around the shaft with her tongue. At the head, she runs her tongue around the purple tip, slowly and then fast, slow again and the rapid licks before he feels like he might blow, whereupon she slowly makes the entire shaft disappear into her mouth.

Chris is staring at the entire event in the mirror, Hayden doing the same from the corner of her eye. Mostly though her focus is on her husband's actual penis, the sensation of it in her is more important than the visuals of the exercise. Chris is enjoying the best of both worlds and loves it. He uses his one hand to steady himself, the other gently rubbing the top of his wife's head.

The hour or so that Hayden manages to suck on Chris's dick is indicative of the fact that she too enjoys the taste of her husband. She makes no secret of this, vocally enjoying the taste of his pre-cum. Even when Chris cannot contain himself, and starts to thrust his cock into her mouth, she doesn't pull away. Instead, she grabs his ass and pulls him deeper into her. He fucks her mouth deep and hard. She sucks his cock into herself, deeper and harder. The volume of the load that shoots out of him is unexpected and she is unable to swallow it all in one go. She gently laps up the remaining cum, an act that sees her husband sporting another solid erection in under ten minutes.

Hayden bends over to rinse her mouth. Chris takes the opportunity to lean over her and nestle his neat shaft between her butt cheeks. She opens up the tub of moisturizer on the bureau and hands it to him. He smiles a very excited thank you and digs his fingers into the tub. He rubs some of the white cream onto the tip of his cock and then a little ways down his shaft. He dabs a little on the rosy ring that is her butt-hole. His finger slips in, just a little, and then out. He slips the tip of his finger in again, the hole immediately tightening around it.

He puts a little more cream on his finger and inserts it into her ass, careful not to put too much or else he won't have enough friction. He lets the finger slide in for half an inch, then an inch. He pulls it out for half an inch and then inserts it again for an inch. He keeps up with this one-inch feed until its Hayden who pushes into him for two, then the entire finger. Their eyes lock as he tries for two, successfully. He fucks her ass gently with two fingers, until her moans let him know that she's ready for his cock.

The seamless transition from fingers to cock reminds Hayden that she's in the hands of an expert. There is no urgency as two inches of Chris settle inside her. They both watch as slowly the cock eases into her. With every inch or so there is a gentle thrust, a rocking motion so that it is Hayden that lets him in further, and not the cock forcing its way through. The view is magical. Their arousal is peaked by the sight of the last inch slipping away into the dark. Chris lets her adjust before slowly pulling his dick out to an almost exit and repeating the show.

His hands rest on her shoulders so that he can pull her back gently onto him without obstructing the view. There's no need for him to really do this, since Hayden herself is practically riding the dick in her ass, the tool having touched the places necessary for her ass to make the conversion to fuck-pleasure-center. She too is in no hurry for this pleasure to end and so she measures the rate of her movements, alternating rhythms so as not to bring on an eruption. She can't help touching her fingers to her clit though.

Chris slips out completely a few times, the excitement leading to thrusting too enthusiastic for the position they're in and the size of his dick. The re-entry is beautiful to watch for both, the enjoyment magnified and prolonged as every slip means not an end, but a beginning. Hayden's fingers settle on her pussy and Chris too feels the stirrings deep inside himself. They brace themselves for it.

There is no need to see; it is more important to feel. Hayden turns square to the mirror and places her hand on it. Her other hand loses its fingers inside her vagina, as many as will enter at any one time. Chris lifts her one leg so her thigh rests on the bureau, then shoots his cock as deep into her ass as this new position allows. Chris rises to his tiptoes on some of the strokes, needing the completeness of penetration that this affords him.

He cannot look up from where his head has fallen onto Hayden's back. His eyes have fallen onto his cock sliding in and out of her tight ass. His head, along with every nerve in his body, registers the pleasure resulting from the action he is witnessing. His eyes close and he doesn't even look up when Hayden slaps her own thigh repeatedly as she brings herself to climax with nothing but the tip of her index finger on the outskirts of her pussy. His hands just wrap around the front of her and he sticks it to her for several solid jabs until the inside of her ass is coated with all the seed his sack can manage.

In the shower there is more touching, more cumming as they give each other detailed attention with their hands. Hayden's fingers wrapped around Chris's cock as his fingers tease her clit. They kiss throughout the entire elaborate masturbation and eventually both of them are sitting flat on the floor enjoying the warm water, completely drained and unable to speak.

There is much to be said for the pleasure two people can give one another in the absence of expectation. This is a lesson best learned in the later part of a relationship, when the superficial getting to know each other admin has been dealt with.

Fortunately, the weekend isn't entirely over. Sunday has turned into night and they will be leaving late tomorrow morning. So there is still some time to put a more solid stamp on the report cards, before grading them on the weekend. Chris hopes that this session will go some ways in improving the mark.

The frustration of the weekend must be evident on her face, because Chris takes the bag his wife is unsuccessfully trying to pack and walks her outside.

"What's the matter, honey? I thought the weekend went great." He suspected what the problem might be, but only had his suspicion confirmed when she started to become a little too enthusiastic about pleasing him. Hayden finds it difficult to answer, her womanhood severely challenged by her inability to make her husband climb the walls during lovemaking. She had never let it bother her before, their lives always packed with distractions so the sex had left little room for question marks next to all the exclamations.

Chris knew that there was no explanation he could give her now that wouldn't sound as though he was just trying to make her feel better, so he refrained from words. He cups his wife's delicate face in his hands and kisses her gently onto each one of her eyelids, then her forehead. He kisses her cheeks and then her nose, before settling a few light pecks on her lips. He stares deep into her eyes as his tongue parts her lips and fills her cherry-flavored mouth. I love you too, is what she responds with her mouth, also a deep sensual kiss with no words.

He takes her hand after a brief moment and runs it over his hard as a rock cock.

"See what you do to me, pretty lady, I can't even tell you I love you without wanting to make love to you. That's what you do to me. You make me want to love..." Chris could have said a million things after this, but they would have been unnecessary. Hayden realizes that she is her husband's aphrodisiac. All this time that she has been trying to make him feel what she feels when he makes love to her has been time wasted. He can only make her feel the way he does because by being who she is, the woman he loves, she makes him feel like the man that can do what he does to her. She finally accepts that she is enough for her husband, just as she is, and that no more is needed.

The warm winds blowing in from across the lake wrap around the couple on the deck. There is a brief moment when both of them eye the deckchair, but Chris lifts Hayden up and carries her inside, deciding that it would be inappropriate given their recent epiphany. He lays her on the bed, putting the bags on the floor so as to create the room he's going to need to confirm with his cock what his mouth just confessed. He takes off his own shirt, then his shorts. The tip of his dick strains towards his naval as he bends over and carefully disrobes his wife.

Hayden lifts herself off the bed and makes the removal of her clothing easier. She has the athleticism to make it a pleasure for him to watch, as she can hang comfortably in any position for as long as he needs her to. Her panties hit the ground just as his lips find her stomach. His kisses send butterflies through the entire length of her and she knows that this is a feeling that he'll probably give her for the rest of their lives.

She runs her fingers through his hair as he makes his way down past her naval and onto her pussy. His delicate kisses show the kind of appreciation for her femininity that she had felt she was missing. She knew now that it was there and that the only person who needed to know this is the man with his lips wrapped around her clit and his tongue teasing the entrance to her warm depths.

She wraps her legs around his head and enjoys every sip he takes out of her.

Chris's hot tongue is strong enough to make a complete entry into his wife, sending her into what can only be described as ecstasy. His almost serpentine stabs are controlled and intense. Every time he removes his tongue completely he kisses her clit so as not to make her pussy feel in any way abandoned. His own cock drips love juice at the sight of the pleasure he is giving his wife, the sounds of her enjoyment driving him on.

The manner in which Chris devours Hayden's pussy is what can only be described as eating. He eats erotic pleasure after erotic pleasure from somewhere deep inside of her. He sounds like someone biting into a fully ripened mango, or pineapple, the juices of which run down the sides of his mouth and onto his chin, only for them to be lapped up by his tongue. The knowledge of this thorough enjoyment of her cunt sends her clit into full bloom and Chris's feeding frenzy into over-drive.

Hayden's breasts fit perfectly in her husband's hands and he manages to massage the mounds with just enough force to complete the overall pleasure arch. His tongue inside her pussy and her nipples being danced on by his fingers completes the circuit. Chris strategically mounts her mid orgasm, planting his cock inside her as he gives her a taste of herself by sticking his tongue in her mouth. She moves herself around his cock to make up for the distraction, Chris allowing her to reestablish her rhythm.

Wide circular strokes bring her orgasm to bloom, her fingers digging into Chris's back as she seems to be suspended in climax. He thrusts briskly in order to release her from the orgasmic hold, the grip almost too intense for both of them. He continues to kiss her as she sails down from cloud nine, pausing only so that she can catch her breath. They lay in each other's arms, his cock soaking inside her, still hard and still full. He lets himself enjoy the stillness of her recovery, allowing her sufficient silence so that she can comprehend her own satisfaction.

The thrusting resumes slowly, almost as though Hayden were asleep and he didn't want to wake her. She was fully awake of course, and she is definitely fully aware of the dick inside her. Chris is in no rush for his own climax, almost rocking his cock around inside of her, not pounding on her pussy for his own pleasure. He gently coaxes her cunt out of its slumber, gently speeding up its recovery from bliss so that they could try for seventh heaven, having successfully climbed cloud nine.

His mouth finds one of her breasts, his hand finding the other. His tongue runs rapid circles around her nipples in contrast to the slow sucking and the gentle massaging. Chris rests his wife's head on one hand so that he can look at her in her face if he chose to. This also gives him access to both her breasts with his mouth, his other hand under her leg at the knee, near her thigh so he can part it and lift her up toward him at the same time. He does just that, sending his cock into her, then around inside of her, and then out of her. They both strain their neck ever so slightly, watching the interaction between cock and cunt.

The effortlessness of his penetration is beautiful to watch, for both of them. The willingness of her vagina to receive her husband is obvious, her pussy practically opening up to him, wrapping around him and pulling him into itself. This moment is what is meant when people talk of making love. There is nothing awkward about the absolute vulnerability of both of them. This vulnerability is made bearable by the love they have for each other.

Taking the leg that is pinned under him, he eases it free, urging her to lie on her side. She does so willingly. On her side, Chris still manages to wrap his mouth around the breast closest to him. He can fondle the other one since his hand isn't required to keep Hayden's leg up. She manages this all on her own, her foot well above her head with no need of support.

In this position, it is possible for them to kiss fully on the mouth when they are not totally mesmerized by sight of Chris creeping into Hayden's pussy from the back. He manages to get enough of his dick inside her for the show to be worth the minor strain on his inner thigh. His back takes a bit of the pressure since he has to almost tuck himself underneath her so that he doesn't slip out of her wet pussy. Yes in moments like this, he could do with another inch or two but to concern himself with things he cannot change isn't exactly how he became such a fantastic lover.

Chris sinks into his wife's neck as he gets close. He takes the leg above her head and brings it down over his own thigh. He can pull her back onto him as he digs into her. She stretches her neck so he has room to play, knowing how much he enjoys kissing her from behind her ear down to her shoulder. She loves the feeling as well, a light contrast to the hard and rough friction now consuming her pussy as her husband is about to cum for the first time tonight. She takes his head in her hand, cupping his ear as his lips and tongue make a meal of her neck.

The view is unnecessary, as the

sensation becomes the area of focus. Chris digs deeper and deeper into her cunt as she starts to ooze juice. She has never cum after him; he's never allowed it. Only once he knows that she is satisfied does he even begin to work on his own cock. Chris is now completely between her legs, lifting himself slightly off the bed so as not to completely cut off her circulation. He has full access now to her cunt, his fingers manipulating her clit. He uses her own moisture, wetting his hand quite completely, to increase the pleasure to her clit. His lubricated fingers are an interesting sensation for her, her cunt weeping with gratitude as his cock edges closer to its own eruption.

She screams her satisfaction, the grip on his head tightening as her cunt releases its load completely. He rolls her onto her stomach without exiting, needing to pin her wet cunt down so that he can get the needed traction. Friction is easily lost when he works her into one of her super-cum frenzies. He does this often and now needs to do a quick pat down so that he can get to where he needs to be. She barely notices that his cock has slipped out as he pulls the sheet up to rid his dick and her cunt of some excess fluid, and then quickly inserts his dick into the dryer pussy, better primed now to milk his meat.

She pulls on the sheets as the sensation of being fucked post-climax envelopes her. Chris grabs her under both her thighs and she lifts her ass into his groin. He thrusts into her cunt with the force of a waterfall and then moves around inside her with the vigor of a tornado. It takes a good twenty minutes of this salsa-type twisting, to get him panting in husky undertones as his cock spits hot semen deep into the pussy he earned exclusive rights to on their wedding day. His climax is as understated as it usually is, but she knows, as does he, that this is just the way it is and that it in no way suggests he is not satisfied with the pussy that has just dealt his cock a death blow.

He remains inside of her, going limp amid all the fluids that are the exclusive pleasures of marriage. If nothing else, this weekend has confirmed everything they always knew. They were as in love with each other now as they had ever been. Sometimes it just takes a little reminder to avoid getting sidetracked by issues that don't really exist. As with any relationship, regardless of how good the sex is, communication is essential in establishing that everyone concerned is still happy with the general direction of the trip and that there is still consensus over the destination.

Hayden understands just why she is

actually the luckiest woman alive, as far as she knows. Where other women battle to keep their husbands interested, she is in fact her own husband's sexual muse. So as long as she doesn't try to be anything other than who she is, they are set to make it for the long haul. She is silently grateful that she didn't, as did many of her friends back in college, try to be anything other than herself in her attempts at college dating. Her strategy meant that she drew to herself someone who was looking for exactly what she was offering. It drew to her, her soul mate.

Chris is a rare find himself. Men are usually so self-obsessed in college that they either become reclusive when they don't measure up, or they become arrogant over-compensating bastards. He managed to steer clear of both extremes. He knew that life was wasted on pining after what you did not and could not have, and that one should rather focus on maximizing what you do have. He made a point early on that this was exactly what he would do.

Obviously, Chris isn't so much of a denialist as to ignore the blatantly obvious fact that he wasn't the best-endowed bull in the field. In fact, he often shied into a corner in the gym locker room, when some guys much shorter even that him was packing some impressive meat. But nature does what she wants and he was not about to spend his cash or his time, or risk permanent damage to the little dick he did have by trying any of the many fix-its on offer. There was just no point in frustrating himself with anything that modern science was unable to verify beyond a shadow of a doubt.

So Chris did the sensible thing and instead of focusing on the tool, he concentrated on the trade. He made it his mission to understand the physiology and the sensuality of a woman. He made a point of familiarizing himself with her body and with the secrets it held. He also took the time out to explore cultures that were known for their generally unimpressive loads down-under, but that had practically written the bible on sex and the art of pleasing one's partner and oneself. Size really didn't matter, as was revealed by research and in fact, any more than could comfortably and completely fit inside your partner was really excess cock. This was an unnecessary inconvenience.

The trip to the lake did something else for Chris and Hayden. Over and above, it reminded them of why they were together and how much they loved each other, it reminded them again who they were as individuals. This can even be seen as the ultimate bonus, since it is the coming together of such perfectly matched individuals that has made them the super couple that they are. That they need the occasional escape to remind them of this is not a totally unwelcome inconvenience.

Just how long they'll still be sharing their living space is still unclear, and this thought surfaces to both of them as they pull up on their driveway and have to navigate around their houseguest's car. But this isn't an issue for them. There is enough love between the two of them for each other and everyone else in their lives. And whenever they need a little special loving from each other, they'll always have the lake....

2 DON'T KNOCK IT 'TIL YOU'VE TRIED IT

The smell of cock, thick in the steamy shower room, along with the scents of gels and shampoos, can't be mistaken. Eight of the most powerful men in shipping are all hung like it as well, rubbing the scented liquids on themselves, the hot water from the nozzles above their heads creating the necessary foam to get the dust off that had settled on them during the drive up to the Hillthorpe Hunting Lodge. The South African Highveld is as dry as it is hot and dusty. Through the scented steam and sweat however is the distinct smell of man.

The suggestion of a jerk-off-shoot-off comes from Jenson, 35, from the Atlanta office of Seventh Generation Shipping. He went to college on a football scholarship and it shows. He is all quarterback. A sly grin on his ruggedly handsome face, a glint in his cheeky apache eyes, his uncut ten inches lathered and stiff in his grip, his large hand moving right over the head all the way back down to the base of the shaft until the foreskin pulls away to expose his growing warrior. The fingers on his other hand feather his balls, tugging at the massive sack as his veined dick develops its signature curve as it reaches full mast.

It isn't long before every single one of the corporate cocks is locked and loaded, all eight stepping away from under the showers, taking aim at the wall behind the falling water. They would be judged on quantity and distance: whoever shoots the most love juice the farthest up the wall is the winner. Of course, adolescent memories remind them that there are usually two winners: one for load and one for distance. Very few cocks have the power to both produce gallons of jizz and still shoot it at any great distance.

The three men to the right of Jenson are Trip, Lathan, and Kyle: same age, same physique, and their cocks all hanging well past nine inches. All of them are circumcised. All of them are enthusiastic about the challenge and already stand rock hard, stroking their dicks to individual fantasies. Jenson is flanked on his left by four power players from the international offices. Randal is from the Paris office, while Jake holds down the Australian front. Saul and Bret are from Cape Town and Lagos, respectively. Despite their offices being across the world, this is an all-American showdown since these CEOs are North American citizens by birth.

Eight Caucasians, locked in fierce competition daily, can't resist the opportunity even in this setting to play a game of mine-is-bigger-than-yours. Even while there is a need for some concentration to maintain the fantasies that are maintaining the solid erections, each of them still has their eyes fixed on the cock they deem to be their closest competition. So eyes move from dick to dick and then back to their own cocks, checking to see how they're doing, and then closed briefly before returning to the competition.

The cock to watch is Saul's. At 12 inches, it doesn't get completely hard, appearing to have a flexible rubbery character. He uses both hands to milk his mammoth member, taking turns in sliding firm grips up and then down his circumcised shaft. His penis is of the same color as his face, an almost olive; the head is the same, but just slightly rouge. His eye seems a little larger than it should be so everyone strokes their own meat with their eyes fixed on the biggest cock in the room, certain that he'll take home the trophy. The slit at the tip of his python seems poised to spit some substantial venom.

Saul isn't as focused on his cock as the others. His eyes are closed as he pulls his dick faster, harder, away from his body, straight out in front of him. It's impossible to imagine his dick has ever been inside anybody, not completely. His girth looks close to six – maybe seven – inches, meandering somewhere between blessing and curse. His cock snakes as his hand tries in vain to get a real handle of it. The veins in his neck and the grunt through his clenched teeth let his audience know that he's definitely close. He's definitely very close now as one hand takes over completely, the other pulling his nipples and rubbing his chest before teasing his pubes, scratching and then pulling on the curls.

The others stop almost, reducing their own strokes as they brace themselves for Saul. His cock seems finally to have engorged completely and looks a solid 14 inches, throbbing, pulsating, and jerking almost involuntarily in between beats. The head, now purple, seems to take on a life of its own, as the slit in it seems to yawn open, then close, then open again. Saul almost stands on his toes as he beats his meat harder and harder, the veins in his forearm looking set to burst. Everyone else just rubs the heads on their own dicks now, as Saul's cock becomes the center of attention.

Saul almost screamed, his head thrown completely back as a steady stream of cream liquid shoots from his cock, then another, and another. He continues to pull on his cock for the exaggerated minute or so that it takes for his load to reduce to a gentle gush, dripping and falling down the length of his cock, which suddenly seems to have assumed a full standing position with no intention of going anywhere. He strokes his dick head with the appropriate hand, the other hand clearing his brow of sweat. Everyone else cums just because they have to, having let the competition go in their mind, a mental forfeit, ejaculation being a simple formality now.

With the loads shot and the applause and high-fives out of the way, it's back under the shower for a few minutes as the sticky fluid still drips from some of their now half-limp fuck sticks, flowing down the furrow and down the drain....

Everyone goes to their respective rooms, having cleaned themselves up nicely inside and out in the shower house designed for the purpose of the post-hunt cleanup. Now in their rooms some of them get to thinking of the weekend ahead. Some of them have their heads on the dicks that they just saw. Everybody has a new respect for Saul, secretly vowing to do everything in their power to make sure he doesn't win the hunt. He can't possibly leave knowing that he was superior in practically every 'man' way possible.

There is the brief moment of 'what if' that a few of the CEOs allow themselves to entertain. Trip wonders what would have happened if nobody agreed to the shoot-off, Jenson having suggested it only once his own cock was already on the rise. Jenson had started to arouse himself before even knowing that there would be the opportunity for a public wank. It was probably from force of habit yes – most guys' masturbation rituals carried out in the shower – but still. Trip couldn't help but wonder how Jenson could have been sure things would turn out as they had. After all, they really didn't know each other at all, speaking briefly at the annual GM and sporadically via video call but mostly through secretaries.

Lathan, Jake, and Bret had the same general thought running through their heads. It's not a thought they would have dared to voice, but one nonetheless that got them from stimulation to climax. They didn't know this of each other though, but each of them had gotten off to the thought of going down on one of the other dudes, giving themselves hand jobs in the shower. They had managed to get stiff rather quickly merely at the sight of the other cocks around them. It wasn't a feeling they had expected to have to contend with in the situation, but the very circumstance was unexpected. Fortunately, it played itself out such that there was no need for an explanation either way.

A deeper thought is entertained by Jenson, the initiator. He had started to become aroused from the minute he realized that everyone in the room was about to get naked. In fact, it was the thought of Trip in particular, a thoroughbred jock, which got his cock growing. He'd been eyeing him from the moment they met up at the airport, and he stole glances at the sexy man all the way up to the lodge. He dared not hope for more than what he got, but at least the images of Trip and his cock, not to mention his firm toned ass, were permanently etched into his imagination for easy access during his personal sessions of DIY penis pulling. Trip would be the game to bag in Jenson's mind, if this was that kind of hunt.

All of them wonder what if they too had Saul's cock. They wonder if it would be worth all the praise and admiration they would receive nowhere else but the gym locker room to have a cock that would never ever fit comfortably and completely inside anyone, except maybe a horse or an elephant. The general consensus is that while the initial ogles would be great, not to mention the priceless look on the face of anyone you chose to take to bed, the sheer maintenance of so much cock would be too much. And also, sex is about two bodies getting really close, not just a large dick fucking a willing hole from a distance....

This doesn't stop some men from wishing for an opportunity just to touch it. Something about that dick screamed hold me! And that's just what some of the gentlemen resting up for a lion hunt the next morning were hoping to get an opportunity to do. Individual fantasies fuel their pre-bedtime masturbation. Most of these fantasies are now related to each other though, and it registers to those brave enough to 'go there' just how frustrating this weekend could turn out to be.

By the time the sun starts to rise over the African bush, the group is already on the hunt. The lions are definitely still sleeping along with most of the other game. Some cheetahs are out though, but they are off-limits, as are the rhinos and elephants. Being in the bush before dawn has a strange allure. It reminds them that there is a natural world that is so completely out of their control that they have no choice but to respect it. So they tread carefully in silent reverence of the million possibilities that could kill them in minutes. The hunting guides have gone out of their way to impress this fact upon each and every one of them.

They've seen no lions by the time they took a break for breakfast. It isn't even eight yet on a Saturday morning so nobody's really disappointed. The day has hardly begun, not for man or nature. So they make themselves comfortable as the chef and his team whip up a bush breakfast, five-star cuisine, in the middle of nowhere. The contrast is delicious. The eggs, bacon, and sausage are expected. But the way that the food is served, in canapés and other carved breads, is a spectacle on its own. This was probably how they justified the exorbitant cost of coming-up into the sweltering bush to spend most of the weekend outside hunting lion that you probably won't get to see, let alone shoot.

Saul goes for a piss as he questions the logic of filling the morning air with the smell of their breakfast, distracting the animals from their routine. But who was he to question the details of a trip that cost him nothing. He would have enough to contribute to the 'what we learned from the weekend' meeting, which will probably be done via conference call once they all got back to their respective stations. For now, there were no lions and so he was going to drain his python.

The guide who has been doubling as a tracker spots Saul disappear down a path between a few trees into the small clearing beyond. He follows him from a distance, not wanting to interrupt his walk or his agenda. He just hangs back and checks that he is the only one following Saul, who has no idea that he's being followed. Having caught a tiny glimpse of Saul's huge cock when he first jumped off from the ranger vehicle for a piss just after the sun came up, he was eager for another look. He watches as Saul goes to a patch of tiny bush at the far end of the clearing.

He waits for Saul to start pissing before he walks up beside him, taking out his own cock. He's not short on courage as he stares down at the cock in Saul's hand and gives the meat a wolf whistle. They both look around to make sure that the whistle hasn't been heard, not by man or beast. "Now that is what I call a dick!" Alan, the guide, dares voice his admiration. "Thanks man," Saul is modest. There is a long moment of nothingness as Saul pisses while Alan watches.

Done with his own pissing, Saul whips his dick around a bit to shake off the excess. He looks down at Alan's cock, a modest schlong with a very nice tip. He notices that he isn't pissing, just stroking his dick, which has already hardened considerably. Saul smirks and then shakes his head, "Must be something in the air up here that makes everyone feel compelled to masturbate in public." Alan doesn't answer, just stroking his meat and almost giggling, mostly to himself. He keeps throwing his eyes on the front part of Saul's shorts where he knows the dick he wants lurks underneath. Saul follows his eyes and then shakes his head, "You couldn't handle it, dude."

This snide comment confirms for Alan that the bait is taken and he walks in the direction of some thicker bush. His dick is still dancing in the wind, his hand still on it, stroking it as he walks to a spot he must know because his steps are deliberate. He doesn't look back to see if Saul is following. He's sure that he is. Saul isn't all too sure why, but he follows the stocky Alan into the concealment that is a perfect circle of bush and trees, the tops of which make a perfect canopy overhead.

The setting looks like a sacred meeting place, something out of a deeply spiritual time where such natural occurrences would have meant a whole lot more.

They haven't noticed Jake, who has seen the entire episode and has followed at a distance. He makes it all the way to the entrance of the green canopy without being spotted. He makes his way around it, searching for a vantage point; he wants to be able to see exactly what is about to go down without himself having to explain what he's doing playing peeping tom. He finds the perfect spot, one that gives him full view of Saul's dick as he turns into the space and is met by Alan, who is already on his knees.

Alan continues to stroke his own cock. Saul looks down at him, runs a finger along Alan's mouth, and then shoves a few of them in. He pushes his fingers deep into the guide's mouth, throwing his eyes around as he does, checking that they are still completely alone. Jake keenly anticipates Saul's dick, but it doesn't seem to be in too much of a hurry to come out and say hello. He just keeps shoving his fingers deeper into Alan's mouth and watching as the young guide masturbates and mimics a blowjob on the middle finger. Alan's dick starts to drip onto the earth and so he stops pulling on it. He reaches underneath it and finds his ass instead. He teases his own hole for a while, Saul still not sure what is expected from him, not really.

Alan's hands pull down on the shorts that are keeping him from the cock he craves. He pulls the shorts low enough for Saul's dick and ass to be left exposed. Immediately a hand is on the dick that hangs with its head facing the ground. In seconds, the cock is in Alan's mouth. He sucks on the meat, still flaccid. He sucks harder and harder, faster, trying for some sort of a response from the penis that instead appears rather bored. Saul is also not giving any indication of pleasure either way. He simply stares at the valiant effort being made on his cock.

Saul looks around for eyes, still not seeing Jake, who really is just a few paces away. The sight of his horse dick in Alan's hands and mouth has Jake feeling more than a little envious. But there really isn't much he can do but watch. Alan is still ambitiously trying for some reaction from the cock he is practically hanging on, but still he gets nothing. Saul remains unforthcoming with any commentary, just watching what seems like an exercise in futility. It is in fact the over-enthusiasm that bores Saul, who has received so many such responses to his cock that they leave him unmoved.

Jake knows that he could probably do a

much better job with the precious pecker and decides to do so, in his imagination that is. He pulls out his own dick and starts to jerk off at the sight before him. There are moments where Saul staggers as Alan's pulling becomes aggressive, desperate almost. When this happens, Jake has to find another slit in the greenery to get back his prime viewing position. His view is never lost for too long thankfully. He pulls harder and harder on his meat, but doesn't do it fast. The sound of dick pulling is distinct, and so the slower he pulls on his cock, the less likely he is to be found out. He makes up for in pressure what he's lost in speed.

The nut sack hanging under Saul's cock is perfectly proportioned to the dick it serves: huge globes encased in an almost perfectly rounded sack, one ball hanging ever so slightly lower than the other. Alan keeps pulling on Saul's dick, which has started to give some indication of life, while he licks and sucks the large balls that taste as good as the dick does. With his both hands on the cock, Alan finally seems to be making progress. But there is a sense that the whole exercise is taking too long and the possibility of them being found dawns on Saul.

He pulls his cock from the guide and gets behind him, Alan now on all fours. Saul slaps the ass now facing him. He uses his cock to give the mounds a few lashes as well. He lets his hands run over the ass, which seems all too eager to have him visit, something that will probably not happen given that they've already been gone for twenty minutes and it will be time to resume the hunt soon. Saul takes a firm hold of the butt, pushing it forward and then pulling it back, teasing Alan with the simulation of the motion of a fuck.

He lets his dick rest on the ass, teasing it further. He wets the hole from his mouth and shoots a finger into it, finger-fucking Alan for a few seconds, knowing that from the pressure on his finger, a quick entry will be impossible. Saul lets his finger slide in and out of Alan, thanking him for the attempts he made on his dick. Alan is already playing with his own cock, trying to psych himself up for the battering ram he hopes will break through his fortress. But Saul just feeds him some more of his finger.

The sensation of dick between his ass cheeks excites Alan, who moves his ass around and around trying to locate the tip of the torpedo. But Saul just rubs his cock up and down the valley formed by the butt he knows he won't crack. He glides in seamless fashion up and down the inside of the buns, his cock enjoying the warm flesh and the friction. He could bring himself to a quick climax like this and then get back to shooting lions. This seems sensible, and even Alan must admit to himself that despite his ambitions this is neither the time nor the place to bite off more than you can chew. It takes time to eat an elephant.

The firm rubberiness of Saul's dick means that even if flaccid, he can start to penetrate whatever hole he wants. It's quite a powerful tool, and this adaptation has evolved over the years since high school, when it was discovered by Saul and whoever he was trying to fuck that a rock-hard python was too much for a human being but a flaccid one that gently became hard post-entry was a trick that could fool most virginities into losing themselves. After a few short squeezes and a steady push, his flaccid head is inside Alan. But as soon as the dick starts to harden and make some inroads, the noise that comes from Alan forces an immediate withdrawal. This is not going to happen.

Saul brings Alan's thighs back by pushing his ass forward. He slots his cock between them and shuts them. He slips a finger into Alan's ass and then proceeds to finger-fuck his ass while dick fucking him between his thighs. This isn't exactly what he had in mind, but he may as well shoot some load since his dick has already been exposed. He encourages Alan to squeeze his thighs tighter together. Alan obliges.

As a reward for compliance, Saul feeds him another finger. Two thick fingers slide in and out of his ass while the monster makes a pussy of his legs. Alan watches the cock shooting through his thighs just below his own dick, which has already started to rain cum on the ground.

Saul's load soon mixes with Alan's in thick cream puddles. The double-barrel ejaculation makes for quite a show. There are very subdued murmurs as both men drain their snakes completely. Saul stands up and has to pull on his meat for a while so that all the juice inside it is freed. Alan, done with his own dick, uses his mouth to help Saul's cock with the cleanup. There's no need to deny him the privilege, and so Saul relinquishes his dick to Alan. He is the first to leave, Alan now taking the piss he pretended he needed when he first spotted Saul.

Jake is seconds from shooting, excited that Saul is now a real possibility. He watches as Alan shakes his cock, packs it away, and then leaves. Only once he is alone does Jake close his eyes and allow himself to shoot. His own orgasmic orchestra isn't quiet and he quickly checks that he hasn't been caught out. He hasn't, and his dick spits a stream of cream out at a good distance in front of him. If only he had had the same mental motivation at the jerk-off-shoot-off, he might have been in with a chance. For now though, he makes a mental note to tackle a certain anaconda once he's bagged himself a lion....

There are no celebrations at dinner, the Saturday night beautiful though. The starry sky and the sounds of the bushveld, coupled with the roaring fires, cognacs, and laughter, make the day's failed hunt insignificant. Everyone just enjoys the location, and after dinner, they all drift into groups of twos and threes, rangers and guides offering up stories and advice. Alan is strangely absent from dinner, probably embarrassed at not being able to conquer the serpent that he himself had taunted. Saul seems unperturbed by the morning's events and discusses South African politics with the owner of the lodge.

Trip finds Kyle alone at the far end of the balustrade on the wooden deck. Even in the dark, the view is incredible. They drink quietly for a minute before venturing into conversations about shipping and their individual challenges. The discussion holds their attention for the duration of two more drinks before they move on to talks of a more intriguing nature. A name that has been on everyone's mind since they arrived was Jenson's, and so they try to figure out the man with the arrogant cock who managed with little effort to get them to expose their erect cocks to each other.

"I think the dude might be gay," Trip guesses.

"Probably bi," Kyle adds.

There's an interesting homoerotic atmosphere at the lodge as more and more of the men start to disappear, seemingly together. This probably has to do with the merging of cognac with conversations of dicks and their capabilities. By 10 PM, there are just three or four pairs chatting outside. Each pair seems to have matters of the most important consequence tabled because they all keep intent focus on the person with whom they are speaking to. The drinks seem to replace themselves as waiters glide through the space, taking empty glasses away and leaving freshly filled tumblers in their place.

Kyle's hand drops onto Trip's exposed knee. It sits there for a while, Kyle watching his own hand, daring for it to slip under the rim of the shorts to feel the hard thigh underneath it. Trip watches Kyle's own hand as it advances under the heavy cotton of his shorts. He gets up quickly as the scene registers fully and makes a hasty but gentlemanly exit. With his advances resisted, Kyle is left to his drink and unfulfilled fantasy. He's drunk enough not to care too much that this could have in fact turned ugly. It takes another two drinks for him to accept that Trip hasn't had a change of heart and that he isn't coming back.

Kyle finds Randal from the Paris office struggling with his key. They are the only two who happen to have adjacent rooms, the group booking having been continentally fucked up by an incompetent trainee manager. He notices that he's as drunk as he is, and so he ventures some assistance. They struggle a little bit more with the key before realizing that the number on the key is not the same as the number on the door. They have a brief chuckle and then make their drunken way back downstairs to get the proper key from the board where everyone is – per the house rules – compelled to hang their keys every time they leave the lodge to avoid the metal and plastic being lost in the bush.

Randal's room becomes the new spot as a bottle of cognac is ordered up and the two start to have crude but subdued drunken banter. It's almost midnight, but they both have enough alcohol and mischief in them to cause some menace. The activity brochure beside the bed catches their attention and they browse, looking for anything that they could occupy themselves with before passing out. The massage service jumps out at them, both for the 'deep sports' element, as well as the 24-hour service on the advert. It seems unlikely that this could be, the thought of anyone needing a midnight massage on a hunting trip totally absurd to both CEOs, but it's in the brochure and so they pick up the phone. Two fresh-faced males in their twenties are at the door in fifteen minutes.

The masseurs Andre and Cole are a little nervous when they are faced with two drunken Americans with mischievous eyes. But in true professional fashion, they set up their tables and have them naked, except for towels around their waists, on the portable massage tables in minutes. The massages are given in silence. They are deep and rigorous, focusing on the deep muscle tissue more than on the surface of the skin. Both Kyle and Randal start to sober up considerably under the expert handling of Andre and Cole, and by the time the hour is up, they are left alone in the room a lot less drunk but deeply aroused.

"Well, that got my dick hard," Kyle confesses. Randal looks down at his bulge straining against the towel and then gives Kyle's bulge a glance. Kyle sees that Randal is rock solid under the terry as well. He is not sure though – now that he's already been rejected once tonight and the alcohol in him left the room with Andre who had handled him – if he could dare initiate some cock play with a not-so-bad-looking Randal. He isn't Trip, but that's okay. If memory serves, there was some decent dick attached to this man who had probably fucked his share of French women – and hopefully men, Kyle thought – in the time he'd been manning the European division.

"So what's your take on Saul's cock?" Kyle is awkward, not wanting to leave but having not much to say.

"I think that's just too much dick, dude. What's the point if you ain't gonna get all the way up in a nice hole? I don't see many an ass tolerating that tool." Randal has his say.

"And Jenson, I reckon he could swing. Initiating a public dick display like that. I think he could definitely be a man's man." Again, Kyle is unable to just ask for his cock to be played with.

"Probably, I think any hot-blooded guy could swing if the vibe was right," Randal opening up the field.

"And this vibe?" Kyle lets his towel drop to the floor as he walks over to Randal with a solid nine inches. Randal doesn't move until Kyle reaches him. Kyle's hand is on Randal's dick before he can speak. He rubs the cock over the towel until

Randal visibly gives in to the moment. The towel comes undone under the guidance of Kyle's fingers. He takes the cock in his hand and pulls on it gently, urging its owner to get up and follow him. There is a bag of toiletries, courtesy of the lodge, on the side table. Kyle finds the tiny tube of moisturizer and squeezes some onto his hand before handing the tube to Randal.

Their hands slide smoothly over the cocks they've taken into whitened moist palms, the room starting to smell even more like lavender and oak. The oils from the massages they got hang in the air, drifting up from their skins. The mixture of masculine scents and other aroma therapeutic fragrances keeps the mood relaxed despite the building tension that centers on their dicks. They don't look at each other now, eyes on the heads in their hands. They imagine nothing but the truth of the situation as their cocks are brought closer and closer to climax.

Randal is first to shoot. He almost tries to snatch his cock from Kyle as his dick squirts a phenomenal amount of cock spray on his chest and on Kyle's hand. Kyle resists his intentions, holding on to his cock and squeezing it gently as it continues to drip. His own dick starts its own rain dance, and he shoots a few streams onto Randal and then to himself and finally drips the last bit onto Randal's hand. The moment is slightly awkward as the cocks start to go limp and the two realize that they are still holding each other's dicks.

Kyle leaves Randal, who is suddenly too quiet for comfort. He goes to his own room and jumps in the shower. It's past 2 AM and there is suddenly no need for him to sleep. He lies naked on the bed and turns on the TV. Nothing keeps his interest and he turns his focus to his cock, freshly cleaned, recently drained, but unsatisfied. There is something about leaving the scene of the crime awkwardly that makes the orgasm less satisfying. Surely grown men could do what they wanted without feeling guilty about it – as long as it didn't hurt anyone else, of course.

He takes the brochure on the table and makes a call. Andre is quickly at the door again, this time without the massage table. Kyle pins the young man against the door as soon as he's inside the room, locking the door before letting his hand find the inside of Andre's shorts. There is an immediate positive response, and so Kyle takes the surprised masseur to the bed. He pulls off his shorts as Andre takes off his own top. Kyle turns him over onto his stomach and gets on top of him, rubbing his dick against the inside of Andre's crack. Kyle finds his cock with his own hands and then searches briefly for

Andre's manhole.

With his cock inside the tight fuck pod, Kyle sends his meat in deeper with each thrust. He closes his eyes and pulls up images of Trip's sexy ass as he rams his solid submarine into Andre, who is convinced that this fuck is about him. Kyle's cock fucks the shit out of Andre's juicy ass while in his mind he makes monster dick strides into Trip. The more vivid his imaginations are of the man who spurned him earlier, the more solidly he sends his dick into Andre, who moans as though he knows that nobody can hear him.

Repeatedly Kyle rams his cock into Andre, who takes all nine inches easily. There is obviously a lot of fucking that goes on at Hillthorpe, which explains why so many satisfied customers come back. His dick is sure to find the furthest reaches of the ass underneath it on each stroke. But every stroke is as robust as the first. There is no sense that Kyle's cock is on the way to any sort of finish. He just thrusts inch after inch of his meat into the very willing Andre and settles into the motion without much thought of the fact that it has already gone 3:30 AM.

It's clear by 4 AM that Kyle isn't going to cum. He withdraws his cock and turns Andre back over, taking his cock into his mouth. He sucks on the dick that starts out flaccid in his mouth, Andre having totally forgotten his cock for all the focus on his ass. Kyle really knew how to send fire through an ass. It was one of Andre's most memorable fucks despite the fact that he still hadn't drawn jizz from Kyle's cock. This doesn't seem to bother Kyle too much as Andre's dick hardens in his mouth.

The deliberate manner in which Kyle sucks on the perfect cock in his mouth assures Andre that this is how it's going to end. He accepts immediately that there will probably be no more fucking as Kyle takes the cock deeper and deeper into his mouth, sucking harder as the dick moves swiftly towards orgasm. There is no warning, not so much as a moan or heavy breathing as suddenly Andre spews streams of cum into Kyle's mouth. Kyle stays put until the shooting stops, and eventually a satisfied grunt escapes Andre.

There is no talking as Kyle goes straight to the bathroom and spits out the contents of his mouth into the sink, turning on the faucets. He lets the hot water wash the cream down the drain, and then he uses the cold to rinse his mouth; some mouthwash follows and then more rinsing. Not satisfied with this, he brushes his teeth. It's not that he's just had cummed in his mouth that has him fazed. It's that it wasn't Trip on his bed that bothers him. Something about Trip has made Kyle come undone and has forced him now as he stares at himself in the mirror to admit things to himself that he's put off as bisexual lust for years.

Kyle walks back into the room to find that Andre has left. He dismisses him immediately in his head and decides that he will put it all on the alcohol if he bumped into him before they left. There is no point in trying to get any sleep, so he makes a quick work of the shower and then puts the coffee machine in his room to work. It's just gone 5:30 AM when he's had his fourth cup and he makes his way downstairs to take in the sunrise on the wooden deck and wait for the others, who should be down shortly for the day's hunting efforts.

The atmosphere is jovial on Sunday night despite the hunt having been so unsuccessful. Everybody has a good laugh over dinner and then stays long enough for the alcohol to do what it does. Some of the guys though seem to want to rest up before the trip home tomorrow, and so a few of the faders disappear. Saul catches Jake staring at him as he gets up. He thinks of going to talk to him but then decides that the weekend has been uneventful enough and it was probably too late to try and squeeze any excitement out of it.

Alone in his room, Saul remembers the dismal attempt Alan made on his cock. He pulls out his dick and takes a look at the extra-large tool in his hand. It really is something to behold, but Saul is forced to think of something he tries to avoid. He knows that he has never really had satisfying sex. He has cummed yes, a lot at that, but the most satisfying climaxes have always been at his own hands. If he had hoped there might be the possibility of a mind-blowing fuck this weekend, that has now faded. He resigns himself to thoughts of his regular fuck buddies in Cape Town and strokes his dick as he plans who he'll be doing first once he gets back.

He is already naked on the bed, in the grip of a full-on jerk-off, when a soft knock at the door takes him by surprise. He looks at the door as though his stare will deal with the interruption. Again, the knock on the door is soft, unsure. He gets up, throws a towel around him, and makes his way to the door. Jake looks at the bulge in the towel without looking up at Saul's face, Saul looking at what Jake is looking at.

"I saw you in the bush with the guide," Jake doesn't know how else to start.

"So?" Saul doesn't care.

"I think I can do a better job on your dick," Jake sounds sure.

"You think so?" Saul hopes so.

"I do...," Jake is sure.

Saul steps out of the way and Jake enters the room, which smells like cognac and camel cigarettes. He goes to the bed but Saul pulls him back before he gets to it. Jake turns as the towel falls to the ground. Saul places his hands on Jake's shoulders and Jake makes his way to his knees. He takes the cock in both hands and lets the meat settle on his lips before taking it into his mouth. He sucks on the head and then takes the soft cock slowly into him, swallowing it at a steady pace. Jake enjoys the soft rubbery texture of the dick and lets it slide deep into his throat. The cock bends and curves inside him, behind his teeth and between them, coiling on the surface of Jake's tongue and resting against his palate. Jake manages to get the entire dick, limp, inside his mouth.

Jake lets his lips hold onto the dick as he slides his mouth over it and lets the anaconda uncoil and free itself. When just the head is left in his mouth, he sucks on it, his tongue also lapping up the drops drizzling from it, and then, taking advantage of the still-flaccid cock, he repeats the exercise of coiling the cock inside his mouth until he is at the base of the cock again. Saul loves the sight of his entire dick disappearing inside Jake's mouth. Jake loves that he has already gotten Saul's attention. He watches as over and over, Jake takes the dick into his mouth and then over and over, he frees it so that the entire shaft is outside and the magnitude of what was just achieved is appreciated.

As his dick hardens, Jake is brought to his feet, and Saul helps him in getting rid of his clothing. They stand naked and Saul takes Jake's cock in his hand, bringing it to a firm texture that isn't too difficult to get to. He gets him to the bed where he immediately gives the stiff wood a suck, relaxing Jake so that he is on his back quickly. After a while, he takes his cock and lets it hang over Jake's mouth, reaching over to finger his ass. He realizes quickly that Jake's ass is firm but flexible. Fucking might be possible.

Saul fingers Jake while Jake sucks his cock. He manages to also play with Jake's dick at the same time. Both men enjoy the foreplay. Jake turns over, as Saul's dick becomes a solid rubber tube. He knows from the brief encounters he's had with this dick that it is too big to stay hard for extended periods, and so he offers his ass up to Saul as soon as he thinks he's gotten hard enough to make a go for penetration. Saul spanks the ass and then pulls it apart, placing his cock where it needs to be. He lets his head disappear first, pausing to see that all is a go.

Jake remembers the promise he made, and so he doesn't make it obvious that the cock has stretched his hole a little too far, a little too fast. Instead, he pushes his ass back onto the cock and takes a few inches into himself before the cock starts to bend, Jake's ass tightening suddenly, preventing further entry. Saul pulls the ass further apart, hoping to get back his thoroughfare. Jake pulls on his cock, trying to relax himself. After a brief struggle, there are a few more inches of Saul inside Jake. Both men sigh, relieved. Jake doesn't want to under-deliver, and Saul doesn't want another disappointment.

With seven or eight inches of his cock inside Jake, Saul starts his thrusting. He stands on the side of the bed while Jake is on his knees on the bed. This is the perfect position, given the size of the dick and the seeming possibility of near total penetration. Saul feeds his cock to Jake, who takes it like a man. His dick gets harder and harder as he realizes that he is being accommodated. The harder his dick gets, the more he thrusts and the deeper he goes. Jake's ass seems to be a never-ending pit as ten inches now slide in and out of it. Jake makes little noise except for the heavy exhalations through his gaping mouth. Saul appreciates that his ass is making good on the promise to do a better job, and as his cock gets harder than it has been in a very long time, he settles into the possibility of that elusive super-orgasm.

Saul stands back with his cock inserted into Jake, watching as Jake now moves himself back and forth on the dick, fucking Saul where he stands. The sight keeps Saul stiff and the fuck fantastic. In and out of Jake, the cock is steered by Jake's hole, which is proving itself to be more than capable. Saul is convinced now, more than he'd allowed himself to be in the beginning, that he is going to have one mother of an orgasm. He holds onto Jake's ass and starts a steady shafting that turns Jake's silent gasps into erotic murmurs.

Jake is pushed forward, flat on the bed with Saul following. He is then turned over with the cock kept in place inside him. Saul then pulls himself back up to standing, bringing Jake with him. Jake holds on to Saul's neck as his cock skewers him and lifts him off the bed. Saul carries Jake, who probably weighs as much as he does, all the way to the counter in the bathroom, all on the strength of his cock. He angles him so that they can both see the entry and exit of his cock in the bathroom mirror.

Jake places the soles of his feet on Saul's shoulders and watches the mammoth cock traveling deep into him and then returning. He hadn't known that there was just that much room inside his ass. He does appreciate it though and can see that Saul does too. Saul holds onto Jake's knees as he lets his fucking take on a bit more speed and intensity. The position has Jake squeezed just a little too tightly on the cock, and it is at risk of losing firmness, the blood draining away and staying gone.

It is soon necessary for Saul to place Jake on his back, lifting his legs and parting them slightly so that there is a little less pressure on the hole. The cold surface sends shards of ice through Jake that are unpredictably translated into pleasure, and he turns to face the mirror and throws his eyes to where there is a renewed attack on his ass. Saul appreciates the relief, and his cock is soon super solid again, his thrusts becoming valiant advances deep into him. There is audible consensus that this is the position to maintain.

Saul's balls give the first indication of a super load. They expand and contract so much that he can feel them on his thighs. He rams his cock harder and harder into Jake as the orgasm quickly reaches the point of no return. Part of him wants to reach down and help Jake with his own cock, but he can't risk the distraction. He decides that he will selfishly relish every aspect of his own experience and make it up to Jake on the second round. Jake has his dick in his own palm and could care less about such promises.

Suddenly Jake's legs are straight up, the back of his thighs against Saul's chest. Saul wraps his arms around the legs just below the knee. He holds on tight as he sends his cock faster and faster into Jake before one final stab that sees the cock stay where it is. Jake shakes his snake until he shoots a considerable load onto his stomach. Saul bites on Jake's feet as he spills his load into him in slow deep thrusts. He lets his cock sit inside Jake for a minute more and then very slowly makes his way out. There is no way to thank Jake for making good on his word. So Saul resolves to give him a few more rounds, making the next couple all about Jake and ensuring that the last one will once again be all about him.

The sight of Trip on the terrace is inviting, Jenson taking the opportunity. He times it so that he gets to him with a fresh drink just as Trip takes the last sip

from the glass in his hand. There is
sufficient small talk for Jenson to
establish that any advances won't be met
with too much resistance. This is the
moment he'd hoped for secretly since the
trip started. Trip is the most attractive of
the bunch. He has a kind of vulnerability
that surfaces almost by accident, like
ripples on a pond that turn to rainbows
only when the sunlight falls on them just
right. He's the kind of wholesome boy next
door that any dominant male wouldn't
mind dominating.

The hand on leg is standard. Jenson
watches for the response that comes in
the form of Trip's hand comfortably over
the hand already on his leg, carrying on
the conversation effortlessly. They talk for
a moment before Jenson turns his
stationary hand into a pianist's, letting his
fingers dance on imaginary keys that are
actually Trip's knee. Trip lifts his hand to
allow this concerto to be played with ease,
looking around to see that nobody notices
the obvious flirtation. Apart from Kyle,
nobody else seems to be looking in their
direction. There's no indication that Kyle
could be a problem. He seems to have
taken the rejection like a true soldier.

It's Jenson's eyes that look around next,
scanning the terrace for obvious
onlookers. None in sight, he goes in for the
kiss. Trip doesn't resist. But he also

doesn't kiss him back. It takes a few seconds for Jenson to realize that he isn't getting the anticipated response, and he pulls away, looking around again for eyes that might have caught the little scene while he waited, probably too long, for some reciprocation. That everyone is still locked in their own conversations is enough for him to know that they've not been seen.

Suddenly Trip is on his feet. He makes his way across the wooden floor without speaking, no explanation forthcoming. He disappears through the large glass doors, leaving Jenson feeling as if he has fucked up and is about to be outed. The last time Jenson felt like this was when he was thirteen and he kissed his best friend at school under the bleachers on a balmy summer afternoon. His best friend had outed him, and he almost couldn't stand the thought of having to go through the same thing now, here, on this trip that was fueled by testosterone and ego. He's soon downing another drink.

The gentle vibration of the mobile phone in his pocket startles him more than it reasonably should. He digs in and views the text message. It's a number: 44. It doesn't register for a minute. He views the text again and takes another sip from his fresh drink. Then it hits him. Trip was thrown the keys to 44. This is his room number. So could this then be an invitation? Either that or an ambush. Jenson is suddenly not as brave as he was when he made his first move. Suddenly there are other possibilities dancing around in his head that could turn this into the worst morale-building weekend ever. This is one of those rare instances where Jenson is actually unsure of himself.

It takes a solid whisky to firm up his courage. The ice melts in his mouth after the final sip before he gets up and heads for the double doorway that will get him to the staircase and then onto what is actually the third story of the rustic-styled luxury lodge. Jenson walks quickly down the hall to the room where he hopes he is expected by a solo Trip ready to be fucked silly. He doesn't knock, wanting to get the possible awkwardness done as quickly as possible if things inside aren't as he anticipates. He walks straight into the room, trying hard not to think.

The room is dark, lit only from the bathroom. Jenson makes out Trip's outline on the bed, but can't tell immediately if he is naked or not. He almost doesn't look - the room feeling as though it were set up to avoid a total exposition. It's almost as though Trip doesn't want to fully face up to what he is about to do. Jenson's experience tells him one thing: this is Trip's first time. Suddenly there is a pressure to perform well and go beyond from simply ramming his cock into an ass that has familiar expectations. He is about to set the standard for all of Trip's future expectations, for an experience Trip had probably not given too much mind to having yet, not on this weekend anyway.

Jenson undresses in the dark. Trip says nothing, and so neither does he. The thought of Trip is enough to send blood to Jenson's cock so that by the time he gets to the bed, his uncut ten inches is ready to open up the virgin already spread out naked on the sheets. Trip has come into focus and his dick betrays his lust for Jenson. He may not have been fucked before, but his stiff cock is sufficient evidence of his desire to be. He makes space on the large poster bed for Jenson.

Trip is on his back, waiting for Jenson to lead the way. Jenson places his hand on Trip's chest, where his heart beats just beneath the perfect pecks. "Relax, I'll be very gentle," he assures an almost shivering Trip. All power seems lost in the bedroom, Trip no longer the CEO. He is now a body craving a first experience and totally at the mercy of the body that is able to give it to him. Jenson kisses him on the mouth without removing his hand from his chest. He lets his other hand run over his body, monitoring the ever-increasing heart rate. Trip takes hold of Jenson's head and kisses him back as though he were trying to hide himself in his mouth.

Jenson lets Trip stay in his mouth as long as he needs to, keeping his hands busy on the magnificence that is Trip's body. There is an almost shy recoil every time Jenson gets too close to his cock, and so he teases him by letting his fingers stray near the neat-as-an-arrow dick often. Eventually Trip lets his lips fall from Jenson's and, with that, his body back onto the bed entirely. Jenson gives him a full glance, taking in every inch of the godlike physique under his control. He lets his fingers find Trip's balls and plays with them as Trip shies away and then looks. Trip watches as Jenson takes a gentle hold on the base of his cock, including his balls, and makes his way towards it with his mouth. Trip again takes hold of Jenson's head in a vain attempt to stop him.

The feeling of his cock going into Jenson's hot wet mouth is almost ticklish at first; it must be, because Trip half giggles as he tries to exhale, managing only gasps through his wide-open mouth. Jenson holds the dick in his mouth until Trip makes peace with the sensation. Slowly Jenson swirls his tongue around

Trip's dick, sending waves of pleasure through it, the sensation new to Trip but fucking awesome all the same. When Trip stops gasping, Jenson lets his mouth slide up the shaft, over the head, and then off the cock. He lets his tongue rest on the head before wrapping his lips around the tip of the cock and making his way back down. Once the entire cock is in his mouth, he lets his tongue swirl around it again. Soon Trip is thrusting into Jenson's mouth as the sensation settles into his cock and registers as the first tick.

Jenson's mouth proves to be too much for Trip, who pulls his cock free just before he totally loses control and force-feeds Jenson a load of his cum. He makes his way down to Jenson's cock without being too certain what it is that he intends to do when he gets there. He takes it into his mouth, going all the way down it but quickly coming off the cock as he realizes that there's a definite knack to sucking a dick. He goes back onto the cock, a little more cautious this time, and takes just a few inches of the meat into his mouth, bobbing his head up and down, achieving little more than excessively wetting Jenson's already wet dick.

Jenson eases him off him so that he doesn't feel too offended. He then goes back down on Trip, sucking his dick expertly while giving Trip a this is how you do it look. The taste of Trip inside him registers and Jenson sinks Trip's entire shaft into the back of his throat again. He moves up and down the entire rod, slowly and deliberately so that he can be sure that the lesson is being processed. Trip is concentrating, but not on the teaching. His dick vibrates inside Jenson's mouth and it isn't long before he has to pull it out of him again.

It's time for Trip to apply what he's learned, and he again finds his way down to the torpedo that seems a little more eager to fire off into his mouth. Slowly this time, he takes the head of Jenson's dick into his mouth and lets his tongue swirl around it. Jenson's response lets him know he's onto a winner. Another inch is drawn into his mouth, his tongue doing a little more swirling, a little more intense sucking. Again, Jenson is generous with his feedback. Encouraged, the novice makes his way further and further down the stiff cock until he can practically smell Jenson's balls at the base of the tower.

Jenson is careful not to upset Trip's rhythm as he pulls him around so that he has access to his ass. Jenson is in a half-sitting position; Trip – half on his knees, half not – braces himself on Jenson's thighs while thoroughly enjoying the practical part of his lesson in blowjobs. Jenson examines Trip's ass, first by pulling the cheeks apart and then by exploring the tiny never been fucked hole with his tongue. Trip almost flies through the ceiling, Jenson helping him stay grounded. The sensation of tongue on his asshole is one that Trip had imagined many times. The actual sensation surpasses all his expectations.

The tenderness with which Jenson eats out Trip's ass is uncharacteristic for him. He is accustomed to experienced holes that require the rugged find 'em, feel 'em, fuck 'em, forget 'em approach that he likes. But unfortunately, and to his disappointment (which he hides very well), he has in his mouth a virgin ass. While virgins have a nice natural tightness, that tightness can be easily mimicked by an experienced ass with the simple contraction of the relevant muscles. The disappointment with virgins was the effort to get enough of your cock lodged inside them in order for your dick to appreciate the signature tightness.

Slowly he introduces his left index finger while using the index and thumb on the right hand to part the hole slightly. The entry is easy enough, but that has probably to do with the fact that the finger doing the exploring was first dipped generously in the tub of aqueous cream on the bedside. Jenson lets his finger slide in and out of Trip. He lets the appendage feel around inside him and then move from side to side in an effort to acclimatize the man cunt with the required expansion. He keeps his finger drilling deep inside him, pulling it out completely and then drilling it into him again, getting the hole used to the feeling of penetration. Jenson coats the inner walls of Trip's hole with the cream, not too much at the risk of sacrificing too much of the friction his cock will need to be happy. He eases his dick out of Trip's mouth while keeping his finger in his ass, he too now feeling like he might just let out a premature load.

Jenson wriggles himself out from under Trip but keeps Trip on all fours. He gives his asshole a few final licks and then some gently stabs with his tongue. Then he sends his cock into Trip too quickly, and Trip gasps, pushing back on Jenson's thigh with one hand in an attempt to get him to remove the penis. Jenson holds him in place, convincing him that the worst is over and that it will just be worse if he pulls out and tries to penetrate him again. Trip suffers silently through minutes that feel like hours of what is actually Jenson's whisky-induced fucking. It takes everything inside of him coming together in the hope that soon this will resemble the fuck he had anticipated in his head for Trip not to forcefully pry himself from Jenson, who seems to be having quite a time fucking virgin Trip doggy-style.

Trip, realizing that the sensation isn't improving, starts to walk forward on his hands. Jenson just follows until he is fucking Trip flat on the bed. Trip is caught between the mattress and Jenson's cock and realizes too late that this might not have been the best move, but every time he is about to ask Jenson to dismount, Jenson's cock finds the innermost depth of his ass that renders him silent. And just as he thinks he might scream suddenly, the sensation does a complete about-turn, and despite Jenson being all the way up inside him, Trip feels like he can't get enough. There is the sudden desire for more.

He starts to move his ass around so that he feels more of the cock inside him. And Jenson, finally realizing that Trip is now fully initiated and fuck-orientated, falls into his comfort zone, ramming the shit out of Trip's ass, much to his delight. Jenson's cock takes on a new life as memories of how it likes to fuck are met with the reality of an ass that can handle that type of fucking. The whisky in Jenson doesn't do much for his stamina though, and so it isn't long before he has withdrawn his cock and shot his load completely on Trip's back. Trip is brought to a steady climax and shoots his load into

Jenson's mouth.

"I never thought I'd do it," Trip confesses. There's no regret, rather relief that it's over and he can now go forth and be fucked without the apprehensions of virginity.

"I never thought I'd like it," Jenson confesses, alluding to his first time. "But I guess it's an acquired taste."

The trip ends on a high note for everyone, even the lions. Trip is glad that he managed to get Jenson out of his system, glad that he knows now that it was just an animal lust that drew him to the cocky jock. Kyle throws a look at him that promises something more, a gaze that seems filled with possibilities. These possibilities are scenarios that Trip had never entertained, and so he decides he will approach cautiously. He makes a note to give Kyle a call once they're back on American soil, and if he is right about what he reads in his eyes, he'll be open to the possibilities. Jenson had said it was an acquired taste, and Kyle wasn't an altogether bad taste to acquire....

3 WHAT THEY DON'T KNOW

The smell of sandalwood follows Jared out of the elevator along with four interns. Graphics had taken on the extra help since the upcoming presentation needed the extra creative's input, the New York based client needing to be blown away. Having wrapped up the presentation preparation, the office was having a farewell/good luck lunch. They were bidding farewell to the interns, and saying good luck to Jared and the other members of the team that would be making the presentation in New York tomorrow. Actually, it was just Jared and copy executive, Collin, who would be making the actual presentation. But it was courteous to thank everybody.

It isn't hard to see why everyone in the

office hates Collin Taft. He walks in and immediately the entire room seems to suddenly be about him. Women and most of the men have their eyes on him. It's not just that the 33-year-old is physically perfect, six feet, the body of a god showing through whatever he wore, and the kind of chiseled features and natural tan that give away his Greek heritage. Then of course, there was the supercharged grey matter under his thick black curls that made him the envy of his closest colleagues. His creativity and intellect have landed the company, A-List Communications, many lucrative clients, and it was sure that because of him, this New York presentation was pretty much in the bag.

Jared is also a very good-looking man. He is not the typical jock, more streamlined, like a swimmer. He's a bit on the short side, just five and a half feet, but his proportions are perfect. He has a natural tan, and has the kind of hair that makes you think of a shampoo advert. He walks into a conversation that has nothing to do with him and joins in effortlessly. Moving on quickly, he works the room from one side as Collin handles the other. They both field questions about the trip and soak in the many well wishes and congratulations.

When they eventually get to each other, the conversation is almost awkward. They talk around the trip and then eventually ramble on about meeting at the airport and going through the presentation while they wait to board. The party is still in full swing when they make a quick escape, each to his own car and then home to pick up supplies and make a beeline for the airport. It isn't much of a rush though with the snow coming down exceptionally thick for so early in the season.

It's almost no surprise when they get to the airport eventually to find that their flight has been grounded. There are promises of it clearing up by morning, but no guarantees. The problem is that they need to be fresh and ready for the presentation come morning. There is a moment of deliberation but then they resign themselves to the only option they have. While having your flight grounded was a fairly acceptable reason to delay a meeting, Jared's SUV had the capability to get them to New York with time to spare, despite the weather. And so the two decide they would take one for the team and make the long drive across the state.

The warmth inside the truck immediately relaxes both men, and once the radio is turned on, the possibility of this actually being fun sinks in. It's also easier for them to discuss elements of the presentation since it's just the two of them in the truck. They don't have to worry too much about disturbing anyone if they start speaking too loud when the excitement gets the better of them. It takes the full thirty minutes into the slow drive just to get from the airport and onto the highway for the two of them to realize that this is the closest they've ever been to one another, alone.

Suddenly the conversation isn't as easy as it just was. Jared adjusts himself in the seat and stares out in front of him as though he expects the road to suddenly disappear. Collin is suddenly absorbed in his mobile, checking and rechecking documents and PowerPoint slides unnecessarily. Both men use the mirror as best they can to gauge each other. There are suddenly awkward questions about girlfriends or wives, talk of gym and dogs, and a rather stale chat about the merits of driving a Four by Four in the city. The tension proves too much for Collin who decides to hide himself in sleep.

An hour into the drive Jared gets what he'd been hoping for by staring at Collin's crotch as he lay on his back in the reclined seat. There is a slow and steady increase in the size of the bulge. He must be a grower and not a shower because the dick in his pants seems to be growing from somewhere deep between his legs. It then points down his thigh before creeping slowly to the side in the direction of a staring Jared, who has slowed his driving considerably to enjoy the view safely. His own cock has also started to grow at the sight of the super-dick just inches from him.

Collin shuffles briefly, turns his head to the side and in the split second that he opens his eyes he catches Jared's reflection in his window, sees that his eyes are on his dick. So, still 'sleeping', Collin lets his hand stray towards his dick. He scratches the general area where his balls would be and then rests his hand firmly on the hard meat. A moment later, he lets the hand fall away, the strain of the cock under the denim apparent. His dick pushes hard against the fabric and Jared has every inclination just to free it. As a guy, he knows after all that there is nothing more frustrating than a suffocating dick.

Again, Collin's hand is on his cock, a mock agitation. He struggles with his belt as if he might actually remove it. Jared checks the road quickly and then throws his eyes back at what he is sure is a sleeping Collin. He dares to believe that Collin might mistakenly think he is asleep at home and actually free his cock. Collin on the other hand knows that this would be a completely acceptable scenario in the event that Jared wasn't actually checking out his dick and might be offended at the sudden presence of a locked and loaded cock in his car. Collin's instincts tell him otherwise and he fumbles sleepily with his belt, gets it undone along with the top button of his jeans. The zipper is next, and then he reaches into his pants and pulls out his dick, just enough for the head and two or three inches to be visible to the now gawking Jared.

Collin's fingers fiddle with his now exposed cock. His prick loves the freedom and the warmth inside the car and it seems to stretch out a little more. Jared wants to free his own dick but sense stops him since it might be difficult to explain why he was beating his meat to a sleeping Collin's exposed member. He also wonders if it isn't appropriate to actually wake the guy and remind him that they are actually driving to New York in his truck, and that he is not in the safety and comfort of his bed, where cock-play would be a little more acceptable. There is after all the risk that they could get pulled over by police, in which case the situation would be a difficult one to explain.

Jared's dick is ready to bust out of his pants on its own as Collin's masturbation takes on some real life. He is no longer just fondling his cock, but rubbing and pulling on it. Somewhere in his head, the pleasure of the sensation has registered and now his dick needs to go on the whole trip. Again, Jared is tempted to wake him, but the sight of this Adonis manipulating his meat is too good a show. He lets his own hand find his dick, rubbing on the straining shaft over his pants. Collin again lets his head tilt to the side; again, Jared's eyes are on his dick. If he was going to make a request relating to his dick this was the time to do it.

"Pull over," Collin says, anything but sleeping. Jared starts, putting both hands on the steering wheel. "Pull over dude, and let's take care of our dicks. It's gonna be a long trip." This was the last thing Jared expected but he pulls over. He can't look at Collin now, who has pulled his pants down just under his ass so that his cock is totally free. Collin takes control quickly, sensing that Jared might take a while to come to the party. He unbuckles Jared's seatbelt with one hand while taking the back of Jared's head in the other hand and pulling it down to his cock.

Jared's mouth opens over the thick cock and Collin thrusts his dick deep inside it. He runs his fingers through Jared's hair as Jared sucks long, deep and hard on the dick in his mouth. He moves up and down on the dick while jerking the meat off at the base. This allows for his mouth to get just low enough on the shaft for comfort without leaving any part of Collin's impressive cock neglected. Collin on the other hand doesn't let himself forget his manners despite his cock finally having lips on it that have been in his sights for almost a year now. He frees Jared's cock, gives his palm a few sloppy licks and then takes Jared's dick in hand.

Collin squeezes on the cock as he slides his hand up over its head. Then he releases the squeeze on the decent, letting his hand slip down the shaft in a loose grip. Up and down Jared's cock he moves a steady hand, Jared already thrusting into his hand, faster than Collin is stroking. The excitement is a little much, the anticipation having been built up for a year or so in his mind too. He can't think of his cock now, trusting that Collin has it under control. He focuses intently on the monster in his mouth, trying to sync his hand movements at the base with his mouth movements over the head and top half of Collin's cock.

Eventually they both find that magic rhythm and the world is lost to them. Collin thrusts steadily into the back of Jared's mouth and Jared ceases to wank him off at the base, simply keeping a firm grip on the cock as it moves in and out of his mouth. He has ceased thrusting into Collin's hand as well since Collin has rather skillfully mastered his rhythm, and strokes Jared's dick at such a perfect pace and with the exact pressure required for his climax to appear over the horizon and make a steady progression towards him. Collin lets out a few very loud 'fucks' as he shoots a massive load into Jared's mouth.

Jared exhales hard through his nose, unable to open his mouth over Collin's cock for fear of spilling the hot liquid that has quite completely filled it. He starts to shoot his own load just as Collin's hand moves the head of his cock and so Collin cups his hand and catches most of the ejaculation. He lets Jared shoot a little more into his hand and then he grips the hot gooey cock and milks it of the rest of its spunk, which now trickles out the top as opposed to shooting out. Jared frees Collin's dick very slowly and then comes up to sitting. He looks down at the hand on his still hard dick, lathered in his load. He reaches into the glove compartment without speaking and pulls out a pack of wet wipes. Collin cleans both his hand and Jared's dick thoroughly before Jared packs his meat away. Collin squints at Jared who is yet to speak. "Are you gonna swallow that?" Collin teases. Jared swallows, takes a sip of his water, and moves it around in his mouth before spitting out of the window. They both let out satisfied sighs before Collin returns to sleeping and Jared pulls off and heads on to New York.

The trip has now taken on a new dimension. On a good day, New York is a three-hour drive away. On a night like this, it could be anything from eight to ten hours with road closures and detours. And now that they've had close contact with each other's cocks without the need of explanation post climax this could just be the best road-trip either of them has had in a while. There is no pressure from the presentation tomorrow either, since they are actually on their way through and they have spent enough time in preparation to know that they can now knock the client's socks off with both hands tied behind their backs. So Jared concentrates on getting them as close to New York as he can before the snow forces them to stop again, as it's done twice already. Collin sleeps like a baby.

Thoughts of Collin's cock fill Jared's mind. He'd been fantasizing about it since he met him and had been wondering what it might look like, feel like, and taste like. There was always such a mystery about the dick because it would never make a spectacle of itself. Collin's pants always fit just right and even his tightest trousers never betrayed the size, shape or location of his cock. So Jared always had nothing but his own vivid imagination to work with. Until now....

It was expected that Collin would have a bigger dick, but this wasn't a bad thing. Jared was anything but self-conscious about his own cock, happy with his eight inches and impressive girth. No more dick was ever needed in all his adult life. He isn't circumcised but a full erection left Jared's head completely uncovered as the skin of his cock was pulled tightly underneath it. Collin was circumcised. A beautiful thick head grew out of a thick shaft that stretched to at least eleven inches. Suddenly Jared felt like he hadn't done the beautiful dick justice, and started to entertain hopes of a rematch.

The white sheet that suddenly covers his windscreen brings Jared out of his fantasy. He etches forward and to the side an inch at a time because there is zero visibility. He turns the emergency lights on and brings the truck to a stop. He gets out quickly, checking as best he can what their position is in relation to the road. Satisfied that they wouldn't be knocked by traffic unless a car actually turned towards them, he gets back into the Jeep, but not before exposing his cock to the sub-zero temperatures and taking a very difficult piss.

Collin is awake when Jared gets back inside the car. Jared apologizes for waking him and explains the situation. "So more dead time?" Collin asks. "Seems that way, can't say for how long either. I've stopped four times already, twenty minutes each time I think." Jared gives the details. There's a brief silence before Collin leans over and kisses Jared on his lips. Immediately the kiss is reciprocated. Tongues lock and the heat that escaped them on the last session is reignited. Fires stir quickly inside the two men and free hands find their owners cocks and free them.

There is no hope of any moisture as their mouths refuse to part. Jared enjoys the fullness of Collin's lips on his own, the hotness of his tongue on his own, moving in an out of his mouth. They take light hold of their own cocks, each man handling his own meat. The light strokes are torture, each dick accustomed to firmer handling. They make up for this by kissing each other deeper, and harder, then biting into each other's necks, teeth pulling down hard on one another's ears before tongues lock again and are sucked on even harder. There is the slight taste of mint in the back of Jared's mouth and Collin's tongue is determined to extract it.

When they find each other's necks again whoever isn't biting into the other takes the opportunity to run his tongue over his palm to offer his cock some liquid relief. Once both cocks are caught in a more forgiving slippery hold the strokes become a little more dynamic. Deep kissing keeps their faces locked and their eyes closed as they stroke up and down their solid cocks with less traction but increased sensation. Another opportunity to lather up is taken and the heads of their cocks find themselves briefly entertained by slippery fingers before the focus returns to the shaft.

As each man brings himself closer and closer to climax there is less effort made on kissing. Concentration wanes as their dicks demand full attention. All they can manage now is to keep their free hand on the back of the head of the other as their eyes move from their own cocks to one another's. The solid dicks are pulsing in their familiar grips, getting closer and closer to erupting. Collin manages to reach over and kiss the side of Jared's face for a moment but then returns his focus to the matter in hand.

Jared's strokes are coordinated. A few long strokes where he takes the entire length of his cock in his hand, from base to tip in uniform strokes. This is followed by rapid circular stroking of the last inch or two that comprise the tip. Quick strokes of the tip and then a few long strokes down the shaft to its base. Occasionally he digs into his pants and pulls on his nuts. His cock starts to spill some jizz, and this added lubrication intensifies the circles he rubs around his cock's large head.

Collin has long since stopped his own full-shaft stroking. He has gripped his dick just under the head and pulls on it as though he were trying to get the rest of his dick out from somewhere deep inside his pelvis. The pulling is an intense rapid tugging that almost resembles stirring at some point but whatever it looks like, it must feel fucking good because Collin has now closed his eyes and disappeared inside his own head. He starts to grunt loudly and then his grunting becomes long loud exhalations from his open mouth. He's salivating at the sensation of his self-stimulation.

Jared doesn't so much grunt as he whimpers, his own cock ready to blow. The rapid head strokes become rapid full-shaft strokes and he watches his own cock now as it starts its ascent to super-climax. With moments to spare, he undoes his shirt. Collin realizing that this might be a good idea does the same. They both shoot long streams of cream on their own chests before their shirts have even fallen completely to their sides. It takes a few minutes for them to recover sufficiently to clean up; the wet wipes again proving handy.

They stare out at the white screen in front of them as they pack away. Then Collin stares at Jared, who can't look back. Collin is not shy about making his intentions clear as he pulls Jared's shirt away from his nipples and starts to play with them, checking his watch as if to suggest that they have time. Coy, Jared tries to move his hand away but then realizes that it's a little late to play the quiet shy type. Collin reaches for his nipples again and runs his fingers over them.

Jared reclines his seat after running the engine for a moment, turning up the heat as well and then turning it to standby. The last thing they need now is to have the battery die on them. There is a brand new one in the back of the SUV, but changing it is an inconvenience they could both do without, especially now that they're getting their dicks acquainted. Collin has obviously had this scene play out in his head a million times because he moves over Jared's body with a rehearsed confidence. He very quickly has him in only his underwear, reclined on the soft leather seat, his back sweating into the seat for all the heat both from his own body and from the ventilators all around them.

Collin remains fully clothed as he props himself over Jared's chest and sucks hard on one of his nipples. He makes sure that the moans escaping Jared are of pleasure before he proceeds to do the same with the other nipple. Jared's thick nipples expand further in Collin's mouth, and even further when Collin's fingers start to flirt with his cock over the tight black Klein undies he has on. His dick is quick to respond to the touches from the thick fingers that have every intention of getting him hard. Collin slips his hand under the elastic and takes the fullness of Jared's erection in his hand. He pulls gently on the cock without over-stimulating it. He feels for his balls and pulls gently on the sack while not so gently sucking on his nipples. Jared can do nothing but moan and run his fingers through Collin's hair.

After a few strokes on his cock and a few tugs at his nut-sack Collin takes the hand out from underneath the Klein's and offers it to Jared, who takes each finger into his mouth, sucking on it as he had on Collin's cock. Jared then licks the palm on the same hand repeatedly until Collin is happy that this will have the moisture required for his renewed handling of Jared's dick. The cooling saliva on Jared's hot cock excites him and after just a couple of strokes from Collin, he is already producing a steady flow of sticky clear juice from the head of his cock. Collin feels this new liquid on his hand and comes up from Jared's chest to check on the cock. He moves his hand to Jared's balls and then takes a taste from the tip of the dripping tool.

Jared's whole dick fits effortlessly in Collin's mouth. The tip of it rests in Collin's throat but Collin has clearly deep-throated bigger dicks because there isn't so much as a gag. He moves his head around and around, slowly so as not to dislodge the dick in his throat. Jared can't stop himself from thrusting and is delighted when Collin doesn't stop him, instead moving his hand under Jared's now naked ass, the Klein's sitting somewhere near his knees. Jared thrusts deeper and deeper, Collin taking it, encouraging it by lifting Jared's behind up off the leather thereby pushing his cock deeper into his mouth. It takes only a few such movements to position his middle finger under Jared's asshole and after a deep thrust into the back of Collin's mouth Jared finds himself sitting on the propped up finger, which slide up his ass in one clean move.

The reflex squeeze from Jared's ass muscles chokes the finger. Collin moves the appendage around rigorously so as to shake the tight hole loose and create a little room for his finger to breathe. The asshole isn't budging. Collin sucks harder on Jared's dick, then softer, trying to offer up a distraction so that his ass can relax. But his middle finger is lodged tightly in there with no sign that it will be allowed to escape. The ease with which the finger penetrated Jared belied the almost virgin tightness of his manhole. One thing was certain, if Jared did get fucked, he definitely didn't get fucked often.

Collin tries to slide his finger out but it proves exceptionally difficult. He has to free the dick in his mouth so that he can position himself in such a manner that allows him full access to Jared's ass and dick while at the same time keeping Jared on his side so that his full weight isn't on his hand and by default his middle-finger. Jared faces Collin and lifts his leg slightly so that Collin can keep working on his ass, which has now mercifully released his finger, while also sucking on his nipples, and using his other hand to tug on Jared's dick and nuts. The attempt to penetrate the ass with his same finger is now met with a little more resistance and Collin swops it for the index. Still a struggle he eventually enters the tight hot space. But any attempts to send any of his other fingers in there along with the now suffocating index are proving to be in vain.

There are a few more attempts before Collin finally pulls his index from inside Jared. He sighs, still stroking Jared's dick though. A little frustrated Collin comes up to Jared's ear and whispers, "You know, I'm gonna have to get at least three of my fingers in there if you want my dick inside you!"

Ever the control-freak, Collin rethinks the situation. He takes a moment to reevaluate his strategy and after working the details out in his head, he puts his new "I-will-fuck-you-if-it's-the-last-thing-I-do" plan into action. He positions Jared on his knees so that he faces out of the closed driver's window, his ass pushed out in Collin's direction. This gives Collin access to both ass and dick, but there will be no more kissing or nipple play, at least for the moment. But having Jared's firm butt and tight hole served up this way means that Collin can play a trump card that has loosened even the tightest virgin holes.

Collin's strong hands move over Jared's ass. They rub into the muscular butt, his fingers digging into the toned tissue. His thumbs move towards the super-tight hole but stop just short of it before working outward again, deep circles the whole time. The hands grip a cheek each and with his thumbs, he pulls the cheeks apart, forcing the hole open a little. It strains in vain to close again. Collin's strong thumbs hold Jared's tight asshole open enough for the tip of his tongue to gain comfortable entry. Jared exhales a loud 'fuck, yes!' This is the beginning of the end for the tight little hole. Collin knows this, and so does Jared. But Collin is now in no hurry to dick up the tight space since he is comfortable in the knowledge that this is inevitable.

Careful to let his mouth fill with saliva so that his tongue is well-lubed Collin repeatedly coats the asshole before him with layer upon layer of the warm contents of his mouth. He then laps up the liquid, licking over the asshole over and over, Jared pushing back into the tongue, which is careful about penetrating his hole, knowing that the tension being built up will serve his dick well very shortly. When he does feed the hole a bit of his tongue he goes in deep, shooting his wet tongue into the hole that had just minutes prior resisted the advances of even his strongest finger.

There is no resistance now as the large middle-finger progresses steadily into the tight hole, which is a little more forgiving thanks to Collin's saliva. The finger makes it all the way inside, Collin's tongue still licking the super-charged area around the hole. His tongue doesn't move off the hole even as the finger moves in and out of it. Jared's ass is steadily fucked by the finger without even realizing it, Collin's tongue doing a stellar job of distracting him from this fact.

The insertion of another finger is timed perfectly. It's not the index, but the ring finger. The two fingers inside Jared allow for Collin to create the tiniest gap for the tip of his tongue into the ass. The hole begins to stretch and yawn at the invasion. The pleasure provided by the tongue in and around the hole makes the two fingers lodged inside it acceptable. The fingers are driven completely inside Jared, who can't help squeezing his ass over them. As soon as the tongue makes contact though there is immediate relaxation and Collin drives his fingers in and out of Jared with the determination to loosen up the manhole sufficiently for the imminent invasion of his cock. Despite its apparent resistance, the heat inside Jared's ass assures Collin that all his efforts will be worth it.

The slighted index finger joins the party next. Collin takes a rest from licking so that he can see that the finger has joined the others safely. He watches for a moment, turning himself on more and more as the sight of Jared's stubborn hole finally surrendering actually registers. He realizes that the three fingers that give a close indication of his dick's girth are now comfortably inside the hot hole he intends for his dick to take up temporary residence in. So he knows that it won't be long now before he's thrusting his own meat in and out of the beautiful behind.

Being the chance-taker that he is Collin can't help but to try for another. His little finger enthusiastically goes for the hole. No luck! The others try to help it but they are already having enough of a tough time holding onto their own positions. After a few failed attempts, Collin withdraws all his fingers slowly and replaces them with his little finger. He follows with the ring, then the middle. This time it's the index that struggles to reclaim its place, Jared's ass now registering fingers in the total absence of tongue.

Again all fingers are withdrawn, the original three making their way back inside him. He decides that it's best to just settle for the three fingers inside him since this really is all that is needed. Knowing that his four-finger ambitions caused Jared the slightest discomfort he apologizes by again putting tongue to asshole and licking all memories of the almost invasion away. Jared's ass is quick to forgive and it isn't long before Collin is fucking him again with his firm fingers, all the way up into his ass with little to no resistance, save maybe for the occasional involuntary muscle spasms that see the asshole give brief chokeholds to the fingers inside it. But these last only a moment each time.

The sight of his fingers in an out of Jared, coupled with the snug wrap of the ass around them have finally become too much for Collin's cock. The meat in his pants demands to be freed. It spits warm droplets of indignation at being denied for so long what was promised it when Jared's asshole finally accepted the three-finger challenge. So while he continues to fuck him with his fingers he uses his other hand to free his warrior, armed and dangerous, ready for battle. His dick throbs in his grip and Collin knows that his cock has none of the patience he's exercised thus far.

He decides to make as little contact with his own dick as possible, wanting to have Jared's ass fully ready for penetration, knowing that there will be no way of recalling his dick once he's sent it into the battlefield. So he loses his tongue in Jared again and reaches underneath to milk his cock as though it was the udder on a Jersey. He slides his tongue in and out of the hole, which is again remarkably accepting of the softer tissue than it has been of the firmer intruders that have meandered up its darkness. Jared's dick is appreciative of the attention and rewards Collin's hand with little streams of warmth, the perfect lube to facilitate further and more intense milking.

The tongue fucking becomes determined sucking as Collin pulls his own pants all the way down to his bent knees. His dick is in pain now for all the straining in anticipation of a solid fuck. It needs to do what dicks do and it needs to do it soon. Collin finds himself fucking the back of Jared's legs despite his best efforts to avoid contact with the hot body that is in fact his to have. There is the risk that the slightest contact could send a premature gush of cum all over Jared's back and ass and this would be the ultimate anticlimax for a cock that has taken so much time to prepare its victim.

Collin just manages to find his wallet. He barely manages to find the compartment that always has three condoms in it. He manages to open the condom and suit up without lifting his head from the ass he is still devouring with his mouth. He continues sucking as the condom rolls all the way to the base of his shaft. He gives his dick a few mercy strokes but then has to stop quickly because he is just so primed to shoot.

With his dick ready now he decides to avoid the risk of a premature eruption by again returning focus to the ass. He slips his middle finger into the hole and slowly fucks it, all the way in, all the way out, again and again. He picks up the pace as the ass edges him on and he fucks Jared harder and harder with his finger. He tries not to look at what he is doing, trying to cut off the signals this visual sends to his cock, albeit temporarily. His middle finger pushes deep inside Jared, and once it has gone as far as it can, Collin drives it in a little more. Again and again, he makes ardent attempts at stretching the hole further and further back.

The ring finger brings the tally of fingers inside Jared again to two. The in and out fucking motion becomes a rigorous shaking and stirring in an attempt now to stretch the hole outwards, making it wider. Round and round the two fingers stir open the hole before pushing deep into it. Forward and then upwards the fingers move. They move around and around inside the hole as they make their way back out. Over and over, Collin repeats this exercise without looking at the ass that he is seconds from staking claim to with his cock.

Again, the index is the last to arrive, bringing the finger-fucking tally to three. The action morphs further now, from a deep penetration to the stir and shake, and now it is an almost scooping. In and out, slides the threesome, stretching Jared's once-tiny ass in every possible direction, the fierce determination of his dick to be accommodated is understood completely by the fingers that now pave the way for just that. The hole is finally deemed ready....

Jared now has no choice but to brace himself for the monster dick that will not rest until it has spat up inside him. He knows that the moment has come when the ring finger doesn't join the others on the next entry, instead what is the mammoth tip of Collin's cock makes itself comfortable next to where the two fingers move in and out of the asshole. Collin has his cock between his fingers just below the tip so that he can guide it to where it needs to be. He watches as his two fingers are sliding in and out of Jared, trying with this other hand, the one on his cock, to introduce his dick to the proceedings.

The middle finger doesn't join the index on the next invasion. Jared's ass quickly adjusts to the absence of the other two fingers and is again a tiny hole wrapped tightly around nothing but Collin's index. Again the dick head is at the hole, menacing. It wants in. He uses the index to push open the hole a bit and try to again introduce the dick but still nothing. With the buildup to this moment, Collin's cock closely resembles a mushroom with his head having engorged remarkably with all the foreplay. He stirs the hole briefly and then removes the index slowly. There's nothing to it, his dick needs to go it alone.

Collin positions his cock over the entrance to Jared's ass. He uses his thumb to massage into the general area as he urges the cock into the hole. It seems sealed shut again but there is no time to entertain the moods of an asshole that has just been spoilt with the most delicious teasing. Collin lets a large amount of his saliva fall over the tip of his cock and slide down over it to settle on the asshole. Once the saliva reaches its target Collin takes firm hold of Jared's left hip and pull him towards him while driving his cock into the ass, which has no choice, but to give slippery way to the humungous mushroom.

Jared gasps, and then winces. It's too much for him. He moves away from the cock and the little that has managed entry is again left out in the cold. Collin goes down quickly to appease the hole with some gentle licking. The licking is turned to sucking and then his index finger finds its way inside. The resistance to the finger is expected but Collin is determined, all patience now gone out of the window. And as long as Jared hasn't actually said no or told him to stop, he decides to give it one more try. His dick wouldn't forgive him if he didn't.

He gets another finger in, just two this time and some serious licking action. He gets the hole as wet as he can, fucking it as gently as he can with the two fingers, but also careful not to forget that the aim is to open up the hole for his cock, which is now pulsating painfully in the thin sheath it has been wrapped in. Collin's cock is truly all dressed up with nowhere to go. He sucks some more, licks some more. He sends his fingers in and out a few more times and listens for the moans that let him know he's got Jared back to fuck-ready status. He sends the tip of his cock into Jared almost as soon as the fingers have left him. Another gasp....

This time Collin takes both Jared's hips in hand and holds him in place. If he slips out again there's no hope of a third strike. Besides, the trying alone is already growing his dick-head with every passing moment so it's only getting worse. Jared continues to gasp. His gasps become steady pants as Collin starts to send his cock slowly into him. Every muscle in Jared's ass fights the invasion, but Collin pushes on, determined. He doesn't stop once as he feeds his thick, long dick into Jared. But he moves very slowly into him and therefore the entire process is one that is soon adjusted and surrendered to. Jared knows that he just needs to bear it until his all the way inside, then he'll have a better idea what it is he has to contend with.

It takes a good couple of minutes for every inch of Collin to be settled inside Jared. Collin can't help but congratulate Jared for taking it all, and reassures him with a few slow thrusts that there are no surprises left as the entire length of his cock is inside him. He then lets Jared settle into the sensation of monster cock inside him. Once he's happy that there is consensus on the way forward, Collin moves Jared back and forth on his dick as slowly as his own initial penetration. It's one thing after all to be comfortable with a stationary locomotive inside of you and quite another to have the train suddenly moving back and forth between stations.

Moments into this controlled movement Jared decides it's perhaps time to come to the party himself. To Collin's back and forth movements he adds a circular twist. He grinds his hips round and round, squeezing and releasing the muscles of his ass so that Collin's cock feels like it is being milked, sucked and massaged all at once. Over and over again, he builds up the intensity of his grinding until Collin removes his hands from Jared's hips and pushes up on the roof of the SUV. He watches as Jared, now totally in his element and having established a cock-comfort zone, fucks the living shit out of his dick.

He had known that Jared's ass would

be worth all the effort it took to get it to this point, and it has not disappointed. The inside of Jared's ass is as hot as it had given indication it was. The muscles that once proved frustrating have now become Collin's closes ally to what is fast building into one fucking mother of an orgasm. Jared squeezes around the cock now and pulls it forward with his hole. He then settles the hole around it, wraps snuggly again, and again pulls it forward. Between this pulling and the cock-hugging circles, Collin is so close to cumming he starts to scream in warrior ramblings and beat on the roof of the car as he himself starts a steady series of thrusts. In and out, he sends his dick, hard, deep thrusts he drives his dick to the extremities of Jared's ass, rewarding himself for his patience.

There is no need for Jared to do any more as Collin has decided to ride himself to the end. So Jared takes hold of his own dick while steadying himself against the armrest of his door. Collin's fucking becomes almost savage as he gets closer and closer to exploding. His thrusts are swift and deep, so deep that he can't even see his cock moving in and out of Jared. It isn't really, just touching the back wall of his ass with its head, over and over and over again. This is the hottest part inside Jared and so again and again, Collin sends his dick to this place that envelops it completely and lulls it towards a massive eruption. Jared has also started to build towards his own explosion.

Collin is unapologetic about the number of times he screams 'fuck', or even how loudly he does it. He praises Jared's ass repeatedly as he continues sending his dick into the back of it, the cock spewing what feels like liters of jizz into the condom that must be filled almost to bursting. Jared has nowhere to shoot his load but the leather underneath him. Stream after stream of cream liquid shoots from his cock, which he pulls down so that all the semen falls in the same general area. He keeps pulling on his dick until it starts to go limp. Collin also keeps thrusting into Jared until his cock starts to relent, exhausted and completely drained. He slowly exits Jared's ass, giving it one quick spanking, a few kisses and a cheeky bite once he has completely withdrawn.

Collin takes to the clean up while Jared concentrates on getting himself dressed. They've just finished sorting out the vehicle's interior, the ignition having been turned on and the windows rolled down slightly to release the distinct smell of sex when blue lights flash into the vehicle's interior. Jared immediately turns the vehicle off again and opens his window to half. He realizes that the snow has stopped falling as two officers walk towards his window, already asking if everything is okay. He swallows hard and says that it is. When they shine their flashlights into the car and catch Collin in the passenger's seat, he confidently explains the circumstance that led them to be out on this road on a night like this. The officers wish them luck, a good six hours to go given all the roadblocks ahead, and they drive off, but only after Collin has taken over the wheel. Jared needs to sleep.

"That was awesome," Jared manages as he closes his eyes and curls up.

"That's quite an ass you have there Mr." Collin says, too late as Jared has already started to snore softly.

Collin manages to take three hours off the trip, pulling into a gas station just after four AM. He hadn't realized how long they'd been on the road until he caught the time on the television in the forecourt store. He treats them to large cups of hot chocolate and for good measure, double shots of espresso. The opportunity to freshen up that is presented by the truck stop is not thought of too long and they decide that a five-dollar hot shower was a bargain, even in the dodgy cubicles frequented by large sweaty truckers. A few pieces of the fresh pie that proved to be as fresh as promised make it back into the truck with them. They eat while discussing the presentation for the first time, Collin still at the wheel.

If they keep at it, they could be in New York by seven, without further delays. That would give them two hours to spare before the presentation, enough time for a real shower, a change and a decent breakfast. So in the absence of falling flakes from the sky they decide to up the speed a little, fueled on by the coffee and pie, and to push through to the finish line. The road is slippery but the Jeep handles it well. Collin is also remarkably good at the off-road features of the vehicle, unexpected since he drives a two-door sports car.

"You know I don't mind if you touch my dick while I drive." Collin is almost arrogant.

"Is that a suggestion or a request?" Jared needs to be sure he isn't just cocky.

"It's an urgent appeal J; you have an extremely good rapport with my cock. PLEASE touch me." Collin pleads, desperately. The coffee has had the same effect on his cock as it has on the rest of him. Jared is satisfied with this response and decides that he can oblige, not needing to reach very far anyway to get a hold on the dick that took his ass to places it had last been at college when he had the great fortune of being bedded by a rather large-dicked Scandinavian. Memories of Stephen from Scandinavia fill his head, sending blood to his cock and forcing it against the inside of his pants. He quickly reminds himself that it's Collin's cock that he needs to be attending too, and despite it being at least three or four inches short of Stephen's monster, it too is adequately impressive. So he lets his hand rest over the dick, already hardening.

Jared rubs the dick under the trousers. The dick strains towards his hand, wanting more intimate contact. Instead, the palm becomes fingers that trace the cock from root to tip, an even more torturous tease. Jared runs his fingers up and down the length of the dick, rubbing harder, then softer. Collin's cock wants to be handled, not flirted with and so Collin goes for his belt and loosens it. He follows immediately with the button and zipper on his trousers and the dick is soon peeping through the elastic of his underwear.

The tip is moist, and Jared runs some of this moisture between his fingers. He then massages the head of Collin's dick with its own wetness, a sensation that has him at full mast in seconds. Collin thrusts upward and Jared lets his fingers work slowly down the shaft until enough of it is above fabric for him to get a firm five-finger grip. His hand moves up and down the cock, a solid grip, easing more of the liquid out of it in oozing drizzles. Up and down the solid dick, Jared moves slowly and deliberately, not wanting to excite Collin too quickly lest his foot hits the gas in an orgasmic spasm.

With no vehicle behind them, and the nearest vehicle a good two hundred meters ahead Collin pulls over. He pulls his pants a little lower, under his butt, and holds his cock so that it points straight up as opposed to the side of his navel. Jared's head is taken and brought down to cock level. He is swift about opening his mouth and letting the dick find a comfy spot inside it. He sucks hard on the cock at Collin's insistence. Collin pushes his dick deep into the back of Jared's mouth and Jared sucks hard on every inch he is fed.

Collin rests a hand firmly on Jared's head, locking his head and mouth over his cock. He thrusts his cock into Jared's throat, forcing Jared to take deep breaths through his nose. In and out he breathes steadily, long inhalations, and longer exhalations. Without realizing it, he has soon made himself light-headed, relaxing his throat enough for Collin to lodge his dick-head firmly in it. Collin plays with

Jared's ears as he continues to fuck his mouth. Jared manages to catch himself before he is completely impaled by the dick in his mouth and he manages a firmer hold on the base of the tool, lifting himself slightly off it. Collin thrusts up in search of the position he was just in but the spot is lost.

Collin lets Jared release his cock completely and resume the expert hand-job again, traffic starting to build from the back. They rejoin the stream of people determined to get to New York by sunrise and make some steady progress. The warmth spilling from Collin's dick gets a few generous licks from Jared occasionally, not wanting to waste the jizz unnecessarily on a wet wipe. He lets some of the semen spill onto his hand though so that pretty soon he has coated Collin's entire cock in the sticky stuff.

The semen doesn't hold out against the heat circulating in the car and Collin drops saliva onto Jared's hand. This immediately gives a freedom of movement that was starting to become frustrating for both of them. Jared gives the cock a slight anticlockwise twist at the base and follows this with a firm upward pull as he slides his hand up the tool. The motion ends with a slight clockwise twist followed by his hand pulling down on the dick, sliding back to its base. Collin is vocal about his approval of this stroke. So for the next while Jared's hand maintains the twist, up, untwist, down strokes with which he beats Collin's meat. The speed varies, from agonizingly slow, to quick paced and almost erupting the volcano before intended. But the variations of pace always quell the squirts, deviating the river just in time. Collin hates it. His dick on the other hand absolutely loves it.

Without invitation, Jared lets his mouth fall on Collin's dick again. He goes down way past half and exhales through his nose as he relaxes his throat deliberately, settling into some serious deep-throat action. Collin is caught off guard but orientates himself quickly to a suddenly very amorous Jared. His throat opens and closes over the head in it while his tongue whips the shaft and his teeth occasionally tease the muscular cock. There is not so much suction as there is pressure and Collin has to squeeze the wheel tightly to stop himself from climbing out of the car and jumping up and down like the kid who got the red fire truck on Christmas morning.

He finds Collin's balls and pulls hard on them as he tries to take even more dick into his throat. It's not possible for more without committing certain suicide and so he raises a hand to Collin's face, which Collin takes into his mouth, wetting each of the fingers. With renewed moisture, Jared feathers Collin's balls while deep throating him harder than he'd previously thought possible. A millimeter, maybe more, of Collin finds its way into the back of Jared's mouth whereupon Collin swiftly pulls off the road and finds a spot in what looks like an emergency stop zone. He can't help it. Jared has taken his cock sucking to an unanticipated level and the monster in Collin has been stirred.

Jared lifts his head out of Collin's crotch to check what the matter is. Collin pushes him back down. Jared bypasses the cock and settles his face between Collin's legs, apart now, and starts to suck and lick his balls. He takes the massive orbs in his mouth and sucks on them as if they contained the nectar of the gods. Collin starts to pull on his own dick as Jared becomes more and more intent on the job he's doing on Collin's sack. The wet warmth sends sharp shards of pleasure through his rod and all the way up to the top of his head. His leg is over Jared's head with his foot on the dash so that there is total access of mouth to nuts. The sensations that are added by his teeth have Collin move back into the seat and up its back. He's caught in a toothy grip as Jared enjoys taking sensuous little bites into his balls.

Completely turned on himself now

Jared finds his own dick and whips it out. He takes a wet palm and strokes his cock steadily as he moves back out from under Collin's leg and rejoins his lips to Collin's dick. He slides his mouth over the grateful cock as he gives his own meat some long overdue attention. He matches each suck with each of his own strokes and soon they are in sync, his fingers moving up over his own cock as his mouth slides up over Collin's cock. It's the same on the descent down both shafts. Jared has synced the sensations perfectly.

Collin suddenly takes Jared's dick in his own hand and starts to stroke the meat while he gently eases his mouth further down on his own cock. Jared knows what he wants but also knows it's probably not possible since his own dick being manipulated means that there is little chance of him being able to control his own breathing. So he shakes his head while swallowing as much cock as he feels he safely can and Collin accepts that this is the way it is. He thrusts into Jared's mouth anyway, half out of spite, half because it's just such a fucking hot mouth and he wants nothing but to shoot his load into it.

Again, Jared frustrates Collin, deliberately, by taking his mouth off the cock that has already settled into a mouth-fucking rhythm that it thought would end with an internal shoot-off. But instead his dick is again left out in the cold, and Collin let's his irritation show on his face. Jared takes the dick in his hand and they stare at their own dicks being jerked off by the other. The hand jobs are not unpleasant and quickly another rhythm is established, and there is the brief impression that they might again have to start undoing their shirts to avoid having to explain strange stains to their dry cleaners.

In true controlling Collin fashion though the script is flipped and Jared finds himself sitting on Collin's face as he bends down and sucks on Collin's cock while Collin digs his tongue into Jared's ass. Jared has to beat his own meat now, Collin's hands both used to spread his ass for full tongue access. Deeper and deeper into Jared's ass Collin sends his tongue. The deeper he goes, the harder Jared sucks on his cock, and the lower down the shaft he goes. So Collin is determined to go pretty fucking deep. He manages to get his tongue inside the hole almost completely, and is rewarded again with some throat action. He lets a finger slip in as well, just one so as not to upset the action on his cock.

"Feed me your dick," Collin says as he feels an imminent climax. Jared struggles a bit, and then lifts himself so that the tip of his dick points at Collin's lips. Collin comes up to meet the dick and then takes inch by super-hard inch into his mouth. Jared's dick is a comfortable fit for Collin and so he starts immediately to fuck Collin's mouth, just as Collin's own thrusts become violent, climax extremely close. Harder and harder, deeper into Collin's mouth Jared sends his cock, getting his own orgasm to pick up speed so as not to arrive too far after the fact.

A perfect sixty-nine, Collin fucks up as Jared fucks down. Both dicks are seconds from flooding their respective receptacles and so the thrusting becomes uniform and consistent. There are moans and groans, but these are mostly muffled by the dicks pounding into the mouths trying to make the sounds. Collin shoots his load first, more cum than expected given the number of times he's already shot his load. Jared starts to shoot his own load halfway through Collin's eruption and within a minute, both men have warm mouthfuls of lust. By the time they're both sitting up in their respective seats they've both swallowed and taken a couple of sips of water. A few bites of what's left of the pie and they make a committed advance to New York.

With most of the boards snowed over, they hadn't realized just how close they were to the Big Apple and they arrive in New York with the sunrise. They decide to go straight to the hotel and get their clothes ironed, as well as sort the rest of the minor logistics out that they need to before the presentation, which will thankfully be an hour later now as a courtesy and thank you for their efforts. They have separate rooms booked but they both set up camp in Jared's. Hotel concierge sorts out suits and shirts that need steaming and pressing while they take turns in the shower. Breakfast is sent up, as well as fresh coffee, and by seven-thirty, they are discussing the presentation and rehearsing for it in their boxers.

An hour later, they feel there is no need to pick apart the presentation anymore. They know it's in the bag. Their clothes arrive and they get dressed. The client has arranged a town-car so they don't have to worry about negotiating New York traffic in the snow, so they have another cup of coffee as eight-thirty approaches nine, when the car is scheduled to arrive downstairs. Collin walks over to where Jared stands by the window staring at the falling snow. They really seem to have timed it perfectly because the storm now seems to have taken on real life. He cups

Jared's face and stares him in the eye.

"You've gotta be kidding?!" Jared thinks he knows what Collin wants.

"I could fuck you forever, but not now. I just wanted to apologize for taking advantage of you" Collin feels he needs to be sorry.

"Don't be stupid, I've been fantasizing about you since I first laid eyes on you. You fulfilled my fantasy, no need to be sorry." Jared is honest.

"And you fulfilled mine, and then some." Collin has no more words and instead plants the deepest, most passionate kiss he can with the looming arrival of the car downstairs. The concierge calling to let them know that it has in fact arrived is what pulls their lips apart.

Jared reaches for his presentation bag and laptop and as he bends Collin sends his dick into him, mock fucking him as he gathers his stuff. "So what's the possibility of fucking you as my boyfriend after this meeting?" Collin's arrogance surfaces again.

"As opposed to what, perhaps?" Jared teases.

"As opposed to the hot colleague my dick has been aching for a year!" He smiles and they both rush downstairs without Jared really answering the question.

It is no surprise of course that the

presentation bowls the client over. The meeting takes just over three hours to conclude, after which there is a lunch and some questions that need answering. Calls are made and congratulations are conferred. At the company's expense, the two are offered two more days in New York to wait out the storm. They have unlimited entertainment expense accounts and so New York is their oyster. The snow however, means that whatever they do will probably be centered around the very expensive hotel they are staying in.

Back in Jared's room they are quick to dive into the liquor cabinet, the mini-bar very well stocked, predictably so. Vodka and lime is the chosen warmer, adding a summery contrast to what is happening outside. Jared and Collin sit in a long silence, each man processing the events since they started the trek through the snow to get to New York. And now that they're here, and everything has turned out as expected, they have to decide what the fucking means for them before they get back to their 'real' lives. Neither had after all thought the possibility of a relationship existed. They simply entertained fucking fantasies, which have now been fulfilled.

That Collin enjoys fucking Jared is unquestionable. Even now, just watching him sipping on his drink has created a formidable bulge in his pants. He has no sense of relenting; his body seems able to connect itself to Jared's for eternity. But there is something else, something more. It's got nothing to do with the fact that Jared is simply a great fuck, but with the fact that there is something underneath the surface that Collin now seems compelled to reach. He wants to own that part of Jared that he senses has never been the property of anybody else but Jared.

Being as ridiculously attractive as he is Jared has never been hard-pressed to find a cock willing to explore him. But he admits to himself while staring at the bottom of his glass that he has actually rather enjoyed being fucked by Collin. He also admits to himself that it's Collin's arrogant and controlling sexual persona that turns him on most. It's the kind of sexual dominance that Jared likes, the kind of authority that would have one overlook any other shortcomings, even in dick size. But Collin has this cocky confidence as well as a super cock to back it up so he is erring on the side of perfect. But Collin also holds an appeal beyond the sexual, one that Jared is open to exploring.

Collin takes the drink from Jared, who doesn't resist. There is no speaking as he stands him up and walks him to the bed. Collin undresses Jared without once breaking the intense locking of their eyes. They both look deep into each other, as Jared is disrobed. Collin gently pushes him onto the bed and leans over him, kissing him deeply. He continues to kiss Jared, now on his back, while removing his own clothing. Jared and Collin are both completely naked before Collin removes his lips from Jared's, briefly, just to check that he's all right. Jared smiles, and Collin takes the smile between his lips and then into his mouth.

Reaching into the side drawer Collin locates a courtesy pack of protection, relieved that it is the same brand he uses, the kind that comfortably accommodates his cock. He suits up and positions his cock near the entrance to Jared's hole, Jared helping him by crossing his legs over Collin's lower back. The dick is soon in position and Collin starts to thrust, not into it, but more against it, gently nudging the tiny hole, warming it up to the idea of penetration. Jared loses himself in Collin's mouth, the kisses so passionate that he is blissfully ignorant of what Collin's cock is pressing to do.

Careful not to ram the tiny hole Collin keeps his thrusts small, his pushes against Jared's ass gentle. Slowly the hole starts to give way. After about twenty minutes of gentle play Collin's head starts to disappear into Jared, who grabs Collin around his neck while pushing down on his shoulders at the same time. Collin keeps on kissing him as he continues his gentle thrusting, easing his cock into Jared piece by piece, millimeters at a time. Slowly more of the dick is swallowed as Collin makes slightly more determined pushes for entry, his cock taking on a life of its own. But careful to stay in control so as not to cause any discomfort to Jared, he stops moving altogether every time his dick gets a little out of hand.

It takes an hour for the full length of Collin to be inside Jared, who has received it with nothing but the light lubrication on the condom. The fit is tight, but not unbearable for either of them. The thrusting is slow, and gentle, as much so as the penetration was. Jared appreciates this consideration silently, Collin gazing down at him for a moment before kissing him again. There seems to be a new relationship with kissing and thrusting that Collin has introduced to what was nothing but fucking less than 24-hours ago. Both men enjoy this new softer approach. It makes a change to the lusty savage dicking that they'll have plenty of time for later. For now, it's an emotional fuck that borders rather closely on lovemaking.

It is only once Collin gets close to cumming that his thrusts become a little more urgent. Still though, he keeps the kissing constant, and checks from time to time that Jared is still good. "Just do what you need to do Collin, it feels damn good either way." Jared smiles as he puts Collin's mind at ease. Still Collin doesn't quicken his fuck-strokes, simply lengthening them. He withdraws almost his entire dick and then drives it all into Jared. Over and over again, the shaft moves almost completely out and then completely into Jared. This gives both of them exaggerated pleasure and Jared starts to drizzle cum from his cock without even touching it. Collin has also started to fill the tip of the condom with some of his own flow.

The elongated strokes also seem to extend Collin's cock, even if just in Jared's imagination. But the way he comes down on to his chest when he kisses him, the way he finds his neck and brushes his lips over it, the way Collin seems to have full control of every part of Jared and the way his primary concern right now, for the first time, seems to be pleasing him, all these factors come together beautifully and send Jared into an ecstasy that translates into one of the best orgasms his had, all without once having to touch his dick. He shoots a massive load onto his own stomach, releasing a series of sensual moans as he does.

Collin is seconds from his own climax and starts the swift race to the finish. He maintains the elongated strokes but the pace quickens. This sensation allows a comfortable post-climax wind down for Jared while providing Collin with the feeling that his entire cock has just erupted inside the virginal depths of a demi-god. He doesn't stop thrusting into Jared, whose moans urge him on, even after his dick has emptied itself. The sensations provided by the full contact of dick and ass are too good not to let them linger as long as possible. Eventually Collin falls onto Jared's chest and nestles his head on his shoulder without removing his cock. They give each other a moment of silence to process.

The Turkish bath in the suite fits both men perfectly. They talk about each other's everythings as they enjoy the process of cleaning up. Then there is champagne, more vodka, and chocolate covered fruit courtesy of the hotel, all taken in the bath. The conversation is easy and even the commitments made to each other are taken seriously without the conversation becoming serious. They are still a little wet when they jump back into bed but neither minds, the heating in the room beautiful and toasty.

There is more talking and a lot of laughter. The two of them have nothing in common except their jobs and their attraction and compatibility with other men. The road ahead promises to be an interesting one indeed and it starts to excite them visibly. The office is going to be the most fun, once they start to let it be known. Collin is mischievous and has a series of plans to make the expose even more dramatic than any of the other gossipmongers at work might have dared make it. Jared on the other hand is a little more conservative, wanting to be open about the relationship but not really wanting to rub it in anyone's face. Collin's arrogance demands this though and so there is a compromise. They negotiate as effortlessly as they make love. The ease of rapport between them is surprising but they admit that it definitely makes things easier.

The snow falling outside the widow turns to rain. It bangs hard on the glass, Collin already finding prime parking between Jared's ass cheeks, his cock already rock hard again, already lubed and sheathed. He jokes for a bit about how quickly Jared gave in to him the first time in the car, confessing that he wasn't sleeping and that he deliberately wanted to turn him on. Jared admits to hoping this was the case anyway. He doesn't wait for an invitation but lets his dick slide steadily into Jared who has barely recovered from the four hours of celebratory fucking that has just ended. Jared looks back at him in disbelief. Collin throws back a cheeky grin and says, "Caution, slippery when wet!" His dick nestles into the hole and proceeds to fuck sexy Jared for another couple of hours before they get a very well deserved and very good night's rest....

4 HAVE YOUR CAKE AND EAT IT

When Tim suggests that they move in together, Robyn thinks this has more to do with the fact that he's just planted his cock inside her cunt for the fourth time with little resistance from her. Meeting each other once a week for sex has become rather an experience, especially given that Tim seems insistent at every meeting to make up for the days of the week he's missed. Given that he is actually a rather capable lover, she seldom complains. He's never really given her reason to, actually, the only time she ever puts up any resistance is during her cycle or when she really wants to see the end of the film....

The angora rug on Tim's living-room floor provides the perfect cushioning for her ass, her back arched off the ground as

Tim lifts her towards himself with each thrust. His cock has an interesting curve that seems to plough down into her and scoop her up at the same time. She found this sensation a little uncomfortable in the beginning, but soon realized that the total access his dick had to her vaginal walls was unsurpassed. It meant that, instead of the in and up of a standard shaft which would provide a complete and rather uniform sensation, the walls of her cunt stroked simultaneously with the precision of the Chinese army, she was now dealt unpredictable blows from a cock whose position could never be predicted.

Tim takes her onto his lap completely now, her legs over his, crossed behind his back. He stares into her eyes making her feel like she needs to say something. She kisses him instead. He doesn't move now, no more thrusting, letting her do what her pussy needs to be done with his cock. She leverages herself by hanging on his shoulders and then lifts herself off the ground slightly. Sticking her butt out behind her releases some of Tim's cock. Tucking her ass underneath her has the opposite effect. She plays with his dick like this for a while.

After a while, she manages to get her knees on the ground, a move that completely exposes her cunt to Tim's bend. Her hands still around his shoulders she rides her man until he has no strength left to keep himself up and he lays down on his back. The view is enough for him to grab her waist and give a few intense thrusts before letting her resume her jockey position. She needs to lean forward slightly to accommodate his cock completely.

Tim offers her his hands, Robyn using them to support her leaning and also to create the impetus required for her to move back on his dick for the purpose of maximizing his pleasure. That he still has a solid erection after three long rounds is enough for her to want to take her stallion for a solid ride around the course, albeit for the last race of the night. But in spite of her best intentions, the last round is a gallop to the finish, Tim not able to hold out.

They collapse on the floor, Tim apologizing in between Robyn's giggles. "I'm serious you know, about us moving in together..." He looks like he is.

"Why now though?" She's a woman, and has to ask.

"Why not now..." He's a man and can't come up with another answer on the spur of the moment.

The hunt is started the next day. They both have their reasons for wanting to move in, and they both have their reservations. But couples need to leap into the next levels of their relationships especially if things feel like they might be stagnating. This is sort of how things were starting to feel, for Tim at least. He didn't want to say it out loud, but that he needed to squeeze a week's worth of fucking into a few hours on the weekend was starting to take its toll on him. He needed to fuck on the regular, and if not, he needed to at least know that he had pussy on hand.

Of course, it did help that he was in love with Robyn, and she with him. But for now, the most important thing was that they were comfortable enough with each other to want to share a living space. And so they took the time off work that was needed for them to make a decent go of finding suitable accommodation for the merging of their lives. It needed to be big enough for them to feel independent of each other and not, all at the same time.

The two-bedroom, two-bathroom was perfect. It was a loft conversion near the centre of town, a rare find in New York where everything in this style and price range had already been snatched up by incumbents unwilling to part with such a 'native' piece of the city. It took them two days to find, thanks to a tip from a friend, and by the next weekend, the lease was signed. It was now simply a matter of packing up and wrapping up their individual lives.

The weekend is all that was needed for the sum total of their belongings to be brought to the new place. And standing in the mess that will become their new lives Tim and Robyn can't help but feel like they've done good. But 'boxes all over the place' is a good look only for the first hour or two, and soon they need to start thinking about where to put everything. Knowing that this could get ugly as the battle of the sexes is always compounded by space wars, Robyn tactfully opens a bottle of wine while Tim orders Chinese.

Another bottle is opened, not totally unacceptable for a Saturday night, and they settle onto the angora, now a feature on their new living-room floor, and tuck into their take-out. A few sighs and it's clear that they are just now taking in the mammoth task ahead. Between bites and kisses, they plan the course, working from the fringes towards the sanctum. They will end in their bedroom. This is strategic because if they do the bedroom first the temptation to sleep might be too great for them.

The living room is a logical starting point since their already in it. Unfortunately, the rug, along with the kissing and wine, has stirred a few other desires. But do they christen the house before it even resembles a house? It dawns on them that they actually can do whatever the fuck they please and deal with the consequences of it all together in the morning. There is no rush for anyone to go anywhere and so there is no pressure to time anything.

Tim takes Robyn's covered crotch into his mouth. She falls back into some boxes, this catching her by surprise. The heat escaping his mouth warms her cunt instantly and she pushes her pussy deeper into his mouth. The light sweatpants are no match for Tim's lips as they kiss the fleshy clit underneath the fabric. Robyn looks around for the single sofa, which suddenly seems too far away for her to get to in time. Her pants are down to her knees before she gets to it, Tim pulling her panties off as he bends her over the brown leather.

He takes her cunt into his mouth from the back, licking her ass and then feathering her clit again with his tongue before drilling it into her holes. Tim quickly makes it clear that this sofa, the new item purchased for the new house, their first 'ours' purchase, was about to become privy to some serious fucking. He pulls out his cock and gives it a few strokes before parting his partner's moist lips and French kissing her cunt so deep she yells out in ecstasy. They both look up, then around, giggling at the notion that they might have been heard.

Tim bites into her butt cheeks and then traces his tongue up her back, to the nape of her neck. He kisses the back of her neck and then the side, and then nibbles her ear, inserting his tongue into it just as he slides his cock into her pussy, beating with desire after its tongue-lashing. She braces herself for him by gripping the sides of the couch, mounting the piece of furniture just as solidly as she's just been mounted. Tim takes his unusually shaped cock into account, and angles himself so that she is not too uncomfortable with the unusual angle of entry.

Beads of sweat fall onto the leather, making the surface slippery as Robyn is gently coaxed onto her stomach. Tim drops her flat and then exits her cunt. He massages her ass before teasing the tiny hole with his finger, already wet from his mouth. She knows what he wants, hearing the process of protection without needing to turn around and see it. He makes his first attempt, slowly, carefully. He manages a bit of his head before he needs to warm the hole up a little more.

A few more attempts and Robyn welcomes all eight inches of his curved cock inside her. Two things about her ass that they were both sure of: one, it was fucking tight, and two, Tim would not exit before shooting his load. So Robyn settles comfortably into his rhythm, the wine making her feel like she was being ass-fucked on a gondola. She rides circles around his dick from the position she is in. Tim sinks deep into her and lets her take him home while his fingers do the same for her.

They manage to locate the shower gel and a towel and make their way to the guest bathroom. A quick shower is all they need to get back into it and do what they had actually set out to do in the living room. In less than an hour, it actually resembles a room for the purpose of entertaining friends. Satisfied with their handy work, they move into the next space. It's a little after 10pm.

It's expected that the kitchen will take a little bit longer with all the little bits and pieces involved, so the couple settles on the floor and empties the boxes of glasses and plates and pots and spoons. Both Robyn and Tim lose themselves in the jobs they've assigned themselves and pretty soon the room is quiet except for the soft music playing from Robyn's cell phone on the counter. After a half hour of sorting, Tim, taller, stands up and starts to take from Robyn what she needs packed in the cupboards and shelves.

Tim's packed the last of the cupboards

when Robyn starts with the drawers, grouping cutlery and packing it in the tray that fits perfectly in the drawer for this purpose. As she does this, the boxes are removed by a rather diligent Tim, who then makes the first pot of coffee in the new apartment in the new machine, another 'ours' purchase. They've done a fairly decent job of the kitchen and Tim sits on the counter drinking his coffee while Robyn sips hers between his legs.

Robyn has barely drained her cup when Tim starts to play with her as he would a tennis ball between his thighs. She dances from leg to leg between her new roommate's athletic thighs as he finishes his coffee. He bends to kiss her, their tongues hot in each other's mouths. The intense heat of the kiss has Tim's warrior cock fighting against his shorts and begging for the woman now deliberately rubbing herself up against it. He pushes her away momentarily and allows his dick to curve out of the slit in his boxers. Robyn doesn't miss the cue.

She takes the dick in both hands, near the base. Gently, she pulls it away from Tim's belly, where the head buries itself because of the curve and the rock solidness of the erection. Her hands are lowered, as low as they can go, cupping his balls as well. The grip is firm but not aggressive. Tim places his hands palm-down on the granite as Robyn's tongue makes a slow ascent from the base, over the curve and then onto the head of the thick meat. She plants a few kisses on the head of Tim's cock before giving it another solid lick, again from the base.

Every lick that Robyn's tongue lands on Tim's meat results in the dick straining against her hands. But she maintains her grip and continues to give the cock a good working with her tongue, occasionally substituting the licks for gentle kisses. Tim's legs stretch and flex as he tries his best to control his urge to grab Robyn's head and push her mouth over his dick so that he can rest it in the hotness he knows is hiding behind the lips that are torturing him deliberately. Sensing his frustration, Robyn looks up to meet his eyes, which are fixed on the action centered on his cock. Her eyes have a cheeky 'just let me do this' look in them and so he closes his eyes and leans back as another lick warms the surface of his dick, now beating from somewhere inside the shaft, somewhere that holds the thrust Tim knows he won't get to unleash until Robyn is done with her game....

Time seems to have lost its value as Tim loses count of the number of times that his girlfriend coats his cock with the heat of her tongue. She suspends him in what feels like an extended pre-climax. The river building up inside his dick feels like it's about to burst forth but all Robyn gets when she reaches the apex of Tim's cock are a few warm drops of jizz. She gives the almost throbbing cock a few more licks before finally giving in to Tim's unspoken desires. The last ascent of her tongue up Tim's meat is so slow it's almost painful.

A few kisses on the head of the curved dick draw a few more drops of the hot liquid building up inside it. Robyn parts her lips as she again pulls the cock towards her gently, allowing her mouth to wrap around it. She has to turn her head, and subsequently her body to allow for her mouth to fall all the way down over the cock that now finds itself in the warm, wet darkness that is her mouth. Tim is audibly elated. Again, his legs dart outward, pressing hard against the underside of the kitchen counter upon their return. His hands bang down on the granite as well a few times before he needs to steady his grip again.

Robyn's lips make a tight seal at the base of the dick, its head lodged in the corner of her mouth. She has to almost stand on her tiptoes to maneuver around the unusual shape. Only one hand is now on the dick as she steadies herself with the other hand on Tim's thigh. But she's not unused to it, and it isn't long before she finds her footing and gets into her rhythm. The tight seal of her lips is maintained, and she moves her mouth up and down the shaft with the same steady determination with which she had just been licking it. Tim can't help thrusting into her mouth a few times.

His thrusts are gentle so Robyn doesn't mind just settling her mouth over his dick and letting him have a little fun. He takes her head in his hands and starts to guide her over his dick, around and around. Tim has the most incredible way of pleasing himself while making it fun for his partner as well. Robyn appreciates how familiar Tim is with her mouth and how expertly he moves his cock around inside it without once making it uncomfortable for her. In fact, she's grateful for the break, having just sucked his dick for almost an hour nonstop.

Tim's load first hits the roof of her mouth at the back, and then fills her mouth so that she has to let some of it spill out onto Tim's cock and balls. He hadn't intended to cum but once he had taken control, it was inevitable. It does catch them both by surprise though, and there's an awkward moment of reaching for the disposable napkins that fortunately were an arm's length away. They both make quick work of Tim's fluids, and then it's off to the bathroom to dispose of the napkins and for Robyn to run some mouthwash around her mouth. Tim always said he tasted like chicken. Robyn knew it was more like bleach.

It seems appropriate back in the kitchen for Robyn to spray some surface cleaner where Tim's ass just was, and also where some of his seed fell. She doesn't expect the assault from below though as her own silk shorts are pulled quickly to the floor, each foot lifted by a crouching Tim so that she now stands with her naked cunt over Tim's face. He motions for her to continue with what she is doing and then plants rows off kisses up and down the back of her legs. Robyn braces herself of one mother of a thank you.

Tim parts Robyn's ass cheeks and runs his tongue up and down the inside. He quickly finds the hole and settles his tongue inside it briefly, before pulling it out and running his tongue up and down the inside of her cheeks again. She tries to steady herself but fails, literally falling cunt-first onto his face. Tim seizes the moment and takes her pussy lips into his mouth, sucking on them, softly at first, then harder. She drops the spray bottle in her hand but still has a firm grip on the cloth. Tim keeps sucking.

He lets his tongue search for what his eyes can't see, and trusting his tongue, he finds the entrance to her cunt. There is nothing gentle about his licks as his thick tongue darts in and out of the little cunt, the clit bursting in all its pink glory. Tim needs a better vantage point, and so he manages to lift not just himself off the ground, but Robyn too. In what feels like one continuous motion, he quickly has her on the counter, on her knees, her ass in the air and her cunt pointed backwards in his general direction. He urges her legs apart slightly and then steps back, taking in the scene and making sure that he has gotten the positioning just right.

He goes for her cunt again, reaching it with ease. His tongue can now skim the entire surface of her pussy without him straining his back. He can also brace himself on the counter while digging into her pussy comfortably, and for an extended period. He does just that. He enters her pussy repeatedly, taking his time about exiting. She's comfortably perched but occasionally feels like she might fly off the counter for all the pleasure. Tim keeps a firm hold on her thighs, his hands now gripping her just above her knees. She receives him easily, rewarding his hardworking tongue with traces of her own lust liquid.

Tim alternates readily between cunt and ass. Both areas are huge turn-ons for him, and both areas are highly erogenous for Robyn. She's never been able to pick between the two having always enjoyed being fucked and sucked in both holes, equally. So Tim is careful about not neglecting either. His hands are no longer available to part her butt-cheeks, so Tim just digs right in. he manages to get his tongue inside her, and then work it around a bit before the muscles in her ass contract involuntarily, forcing him to exit. He's undeterred and repeats the endeavor a few more times, offering her maximum pleasure in the rear before making his way back to the front. Her pussy is happy to have him back on it when his tongue eventually finds the entrance to her vagina again.

He licks the inside walls of her cunt as though he were painting it a different color. She starts to pant as his tongue manages to get deep enough inside her to unsettle her g-spot. She parts her legs a little more, an effort to get that particular spot hit again. He does, but sporadically. She can't build a momentum with his lick varying too much in depth and intensity. This is going to be an unusual climax, if not just for the fact that she doesn't sense it approaching at all. Her cunt is in the throes of a super-muff no doubt. But her g-spot is suffering from a crisis of identity as Tim's tongue misses it more times that he hits it. Part of her just wants to ask him to fuck her already, the frustration almost unbearable. But he seems to need her to let him be.

Robyn parts her legs a little more; she's almost flat on the counter now. Tim raises her a bit, as he loses access to her pussy. He takes a few more stabs at the vagina, inside it, and then replaces his tongue immediately with two fingers. His tongue finds her ass again as his fingers now make a slow and deliberate search for her neglected g-spot. Robyn lets him know when he's found it and he goes to work. His tongue doesn't skip a beat in her butt-hole as his fingers finally get her cunt into such a state it starts to run pussy-poison all over his hand. Still his fingers dig deeper and deeper inside her. More and more juice gushes out.

The closer Robyn gets to orgasm the louder she becomes. Tim takes this cue and fingers her more quickly, deeper and harder too. He stirs the inner walls of her cunt as she finally arches back towards him and then lets her cunt fall onto his hand as his fingers make her circle a little bigger. She reaches for his hand and holds it in place as she fucks his fingers herself for a few final moments before eventually collapsing to the counter. Tim is slow about his exit as usual, not wanting to leave her too vacant too soon. He licks up the excess cunt juice around her pussy and then licks her clit and cunt gently as Robyn rocks herself back from cloud nine.

It's a little after midnight when they walk into the guest bedroom, the next room that requires attention. Robyn has Tim's t-shirt on and nothing else. Tim just has his boxers on. They make the bed and then start to pack their excess bits and pieces in the cupboards. Linen and sports equipment mostly goes into the impressive storage space in the guest room. It takes them little over an hour to be done with this room. They both look over at the made bed, inviting after all the sex, wine and unpacking. They exchange a look between themselves that says 'it would be great, just for a few minutes'. They're spooning on the bed instantly.

They both fall into a light sleep that lasts only as long as it takes for Tim's dick to register that mouth isn't pussy and while he's just had an awesome blowjob; that was nothing compared to what lay nestled between Robyn's thighs. He lifts the t-shirt up above her ass and gives the perfect booty a long look that translates immediately into a rock-hard erection. Again, he makes use of the slit in the front of his shorts and frees his dick through the window. He lets the bend settle between Robyn's ass cheeks, a move that wakes her immediately. She pushes back against his cock and relaxes into whatever Tim's agenda might be.

Tim's shaft moves up and down the inside walls of Robyn's behind. The head of his cock again is closer to his own navel than it is to any of Robyn's holes. He pushes forward, and then pulls back, forward and backwards, forward and backwards, his forward thrusts increasing in power with each stroke. She compliments his motion with a circular gyration of her own. She clenches her cheeks tightly and works the shaft trapped between them. Tim starts to thrust higher and higher up until each stroke ends with his balls touching the base of Robyn's butt-cheeks and the head of his cock is in the vicinity of her asshole on the reverse. She feels the sticky lubricating jizz coming from the head of his cock with these new elongated strokes, and soon he starts to indicate what he intends to do with his self-lubricated saber.

Tim takes his cock in hand and lets it settle near Robyn's asshole. Using his own fingers to hold the tool steady, he makes slow attempts at the hole. Each attempt results in involuntary contractions from Robyn, who always has this initial response. There is no rush and Tim just lets his cock circle the hole, rubbing against the heat of the hole that's almost ready to receive him. His cock spits a few more drops of pre-cum and Tim takes this opportunity to get his head inside the hole. Robyn immediately reaches back and places a hand on his thigh to halt further entry. Tim places a hand on her hip and holds her in place as his cock is gripped tightly by her ass, now squeezing tightly around his purple head.

Slowly, he pulls Robyn back onto his dick, stopping briefly whenever she resists. As soon as her resistance ceases, he pulls her back a little more, his cock disappearing slowly into her ass. The thickest part of Tim's dick is at the middle of the shaft where the bend is and once this part of his penis is nestled inside tight little Robyn Tim knows that it's A for away. He makes a few short quick digs into her ass before a long slow one, a couple more short stabs, then a long one. Each long stroke takes him deeper into Robyn who now has pulled her knees to her chest to facilitate entry. Tim lets his available arm slip between her legs and then lets his hand grasp the knee and assist with keeping it up near her breasts. He is also able to lift and part her legs at will now.

Still, there is no urgency as Tim has free reign of the ass enveloping his cock. He keeps his woman in mind with every stroke, taking her pleasure into consideration, keeping his thrusts gentle, sure to extract a moan on each movement. Robyn lets her ass dance around the cock inside her as she finally warms up completely and is adequately lubricated by Tim's pre-load. Her own movements let Tim know that he has more room to play now because all tension has dissipated and Robyn's ass is fuck-ready. He releases his hand from between her thighs and coaxes her onto her stomach.

Tim props himself up on both hands and watches his dick slip in and out of Robyn as she seems to fuck the bed and lift her ass to swallow more dick at the same time. He watches this scene that sends fire to his already hell-hot cock and allows her to build up her inner volcano as well. He lets his dick dip completely inside her, slides his hands under her arms at the shoulder and pulls her down as she pushes her ass up simultaneously. Tim now has his curved cock completely inside Robyn. He kisses the side of her neck as he sends his cock in and out of her with a greater determination now that she's let him in all the way. He has now lost himself in the pleasure of fucking the shit out of her.

Robyn keeps her ass slightly lifted off the bed now so that Tim can plough deep inside her. She too has lost herself to the pounding her ass is getting. Lifting her ass also allows her to slide her hands between her own legs and attend to what has become a dripping cunt. She digs into herself and starts to work her own pussy as Tim deals with her other happy place. The sickle shape of the dick inside her literally hooks her and lifts her as it slides in and out of her. Occasionally, she makes the necessary adjustments when the angle becomes awkward, but for the most part, they've both past any discomfort and make their way to the finish line. There is no deeper left for Tim to go so he goes harder. Robyn treats her cunt to some DIY as her ass gets maximum thrust from the savage inside it.

In her ass, Tim's cock sways from side to side in between thrusts. He goes inside her until his hipbone rests on the mounds of her beautiful behind, and then lets his dick settle as he sways his hips from side to side. This gives Robyn a moment or two to focus on her fingers in her pussy, her clit also getting tangible treatments from her moist fingertips. She fingers herself almost as hard as Tim fucks her, digging deeper and deeper into her own vagina, contorting herself upwards against Tim's hipbones, his dick locked firmly in place. She finds every possible angle that will allow for her to totally ravage her cunt without losing the angle of vantage established for Tim's fantastic fuck-stick.

Again, Tim's hands hold him up so that

he can increase the surface area of his own pleasure. His cock now slides almost completely out before digging all the way back in. He keeps these long strokes steady so as not to slip out of Robyn completely, since this would mean the effort of reentering her. She also knows not to make any sudden movements, and for the moment, she releases her cunt from her own grip. Her pussy screams at this neglect, but every strong stroke that ends with the curved cock in the far reaches of her ass appeases it. Tim has every intention now of reaching a mind-blowing orgasm as he starts to dig into Robyn at an angle. He uses just one hand now to hold himself up as the other hand pulls one of Robyn's butt-cheeks to the side. This opens her up by a few millimeters more, but this is enough for the new angular fucking to be comfortable for them both. Tim fucks her harder and harder, Robyn starting to move away from his cock as his strokes become more determined. He can't afford to lose her now so he mounts her again directly from above and sinks his dick into her depths once more. She moans loudly as his hips rest again on her cheeks. He's all the way inside her again.

This time, he takes his hands and finds her cunt. He lifts her into his cock while sending a few of his fingers into her hungry vagina. He pulls her pussy apart and fills it with as many fingers as he can reach into her without breaking his wrists. She reaches for the pillows and pulls them to her face, muffling the sound of her screams as Tim devours ass and cunt with the savageness of a hungry lion. His fingers are deep in her cunt, stabbing in and out, pulling the walls of her pussy apart and then drilling into the hole. Her ass is pounded rigorously, each stroke sending her further and further towards orgasm. Tim is on to her climax and senses that the wetness on his hands is an indication that now would be a good time to take her there. He sends his cock deep into her, again and again, relentlessly fucking the tiny little hole. Robyn screams as her pussy spills rivers of heat all over the new sheets.

Satisfied that Robyn is sorted, he takes her thighs in hand from underneath and parts them so that her own hands once again find her cunt and settle there to bring it slowly back from where Tim's just taken it. She knows that it's all about him now, and so she braces herself as his dick starts to push hard against the insides of her ass in an effort to relieve itself. He grips her thighs hard, so hard that she's sure his fingers will leave an imprint. But the skill with which he fucks her makes any bedroom battle scars worth it. The long tool moves in and out of her, as far out as is possible with Tim having gone so deep. His long strokes are soon replaced by shorter and shorter jabs. Faster and faster, Tim fucks Robyn's ass in ever-shorter strokes. It is with these short swift strokes that he eventually brings himself to his own finish, the first stream of cum already escaping his cock as he withdraws, the second stream spraying all over her back, along with every subsequent stream.

Again, he sandwiches his cock between her cheeks and gives a few strokes just to get the last of the juices out. He falls onto her, nestling into his own warmth now mixed with her sweat. They take a moment to enjoy what was fucking fantastic sex before they start to cool down, making the shower very inviting. Wet and sticky they again make their way to the guest bathroom where the shower cubicle is big enough for four. The hot water is welcome over their exhausted bodies and they take their time soaking up the warmth before even thinking of cleaning up. Once they've showered up, they both sit themselves down on the floor of the large shower and simply enjoy the moment.

Robyn rests her head on Tim's shoulders, and they brush each others hair as the water rains down on them.

They spend a long time kissing and an even longer time talking. It is clear to both of them that this was a very good idea indeed. Not just for the sex mind you, but for the fact that they had access to each other at opportune times like this, almost five in the morning, to just sit in the shower and talk about anything they had on their minds. The moment is beautiful, and they are determined now more than ever to make as many of these moments as they can. After all, this was their house, and whatever they said went. Tim spots Robyn's cunt as she tries to curl up to him under the warmth and again his cock is reminded that ass too isn't pussy....

Tim walks his fingers up and down Robyn's legs. She looks at his hard dick and shakes her head in disbelief. He smiles at her, blaming her for the erection. He lets his fingers play with her belly button, and she parts her legs teasingly. He takes the gap and rests his palm over her pussy. He plays a game of peek-a-boo with her cunt that soon has Robyn in stitches. There really is much to be said for couples shacking up together. The merits speak for themselves.

The warmth in the shower has every muscle in Robyn's body completely relaxed, despite their lack of sleep and jackrabbit fucking. So it is easy for Tim to move her around like a ragdoll. She is literally putty in his hands. He props her up on the side of the shower that faces the spout, and then he directs the nozzle so that the jets pulse directly onto her cunt. Her knees are lifted so that her feet are flat on the detailed mosaic and Tim rests his one hand on the knee closest to him so that he can keep her legs as wide open as he'd like them. For a moment, he watches the water rain on the cunt that must itself already be moistening from the inside in anticipation of what might be coming. If the look on his face is anything to go by, Tim has a few surprises in store for Robyn's pussy.

She watches as Tim teases her cunt with his index finger. He dips the finger into her slightly, then lets it sit there for a while, threatens to push it in but then pulls it out instead. He does the same with his middle finger, licking whichever finger he inserts into her vagina, closing his eyes as he sucks on the finger, signaling his enjoyment of her taste. His middle finger is the member of choice as he lets it find her pussy again. Again, he lets it linger. This time the mock entry is a mock exit, and Robyn closes her eyes as the finger creeps all the way inside her. The fist formed by the other fingers push against the outside walls of her vagina.

She expects a withdrawal but he just keeps his finger where it is. Her eyes open to catch him staring at her face, smiling. She smiles back just as the finger inside her pussy starts to move. But it isn't moving out of her. The thick finger is moving around and around inside of her. Tim has turned his finger into a hand-mixer, and Robyn's vagina has become the mixing bowl. He keeps whisking the inside of her wet vagina as he plants his lips on hers. The kiss is both long and passionate; ending as Tim finally pulls the finger from her cunt, not losing the circular whisks until he has exited completely.

Tim's mouth finds Robyn's cunt, the water from the shower now hitting the back of his head. He angles his head so that the water runs off his face and not into it. He can now sink his tongue into her pussy without drowning. Robyn is grateful for the back support offered by the shower wall and pushes herself into it as Tim digs into her. His tongue is insistent on tasting every corner of her cunt and so Tim gets very creative with the positioning of his body so that he can get all the way in there. By the time he settles into the pussy in his mouth he is lying on his side with his knees pulled up almost in the fetal position and Robyn's one leg pulled over his head. He can now cover her vagina with his tongue before sending it into her. She gasps as the tongue slithers into her depths and then out again, licking her clit before slithering back inside her again.

Coming up for air, he notices that Robyn's cunt has started to beat visibly, requiring more solid attention. He stands her up and sends a finger into her from below. He follows this immediately with another. Two fingers move in and out of her pussy as he comes up and finds her clit again. His tongue assaults the pink bud while his fingers coax the muscles inside her cunt to action. They wrap and release with each entry. Her cunt very quickly becomes possessive of his fingers. On his knees, he is comfortable enough to stay in this position for as long as it takes. Robyn braces herself on Tim's head as he settles into a steady combination of licking and fingering that quickly sends her to her tiptoes again. He always manages to get her to reach for the stars.

Tim adds a third finger as he makes his way up off the floor. He gives her clit a few farewell kisses and starts to plant his lips up the side of her belly. He reaches her breasts, taking them into his mouth in sequence as his fingers fill her vagina completely. He doesn't withdraw them as he sucks gently on her nipples. Tim instead repeats the circle action his middle finger earlier introduced. This time though this circular motion is coupled with a 'calling' gesture, his three fingers moving back and forth inside her as though he were calling someone somewhere behind her. His lips get to her neck. He's now standing almost straight and so he has to almost lift her slightly forward and upward using the leverage he has on her vagina. She moves with him, allowing him to do what he wants with her as their lips finally meet and fucking becomes lovemaking.

Their lips don't part as Tim replaces his fingers with his cock. He holds on to his dick around the middle and pushes it into Robyn. He pulls it out completely shortly after. Again, he enters her, only to where his fingers grip his dick, mid-shaft, keeps it there without moving and then again withdraws. Over and over, he keeps feeding her his dick like this, building her desire to have it inside her, doing what it is known to do so well. Inside her, again he releases his hand, taking both Robyn's hands in his palms and raising them above her head.

Caught between a cock and a hard place, Robyn lets herself be taken. Tim brings his legs together between hers and then parts his legs so that her thighs can rest on his knees. He thrusts into her now completely and doesn't exit at all because of the position they're in. Basically, Tim is leveraging Robyn's weight in order to keep his dick inside her. The result of this is that his thrusts take his cock all the way inside her, and what would have been a reverse thrust or a withdrawal is more like dick pressure against the walls of her pussy. Both of them receive incredible pleasure with every movement, both voluntary and not.

Tim straightens up again, pinning Robyn to the shower wall and lifting her off the ground. He takes her legs around his waist and grabs hold of her ass as she grabs onto his neck. His waist moves in small circles, his cock doing the same inside Robyn. He raises and lowers her repeatedly on his dick, the water still jetting down over them. Up and down, Robyn is guided on the cock that has not once given any indication of losing steam. She wraps tightly around his waist and squeezes her pussy around the dick, adding to the intensity of the pleasure and the pressure. Again, they kiss, and again it is long, passionate and deep.

With Robyn tight around his cock, Tim again starts to move in and out of her. His movements out of her are slow, the squeeze on his cock delicious. His penetration is equally slow, the resistance put up by her cunt also making for a rather pleasurable challenge. Slow in, slow out, slow in and even more slowly out, the new snail-pace of their lovemaking adding to every sensation, heightening every emotion. This is not about climax; cumming doesn't seem to be on the agenda. Tim now just makes his woman and himself feel as good as they can both possibly feel wrapped around each other. He kisses her as though her tongue holds the answers to all his questions. He makes love to her as though her pussy holds the secrets to all his desires.

After what feels like a million forevers, Tim lifts Robyn completely off his penis and places her gently on the floor. He closes the taps and walks her out of the cubicle, which has remained remarkably warm the whole time. The sun shining into the bathroom lets them know that it must be around seven AM at least. Tim dries Robyn and himself. He then lathers her with a variety of lotions that he's seen her use. She starts to smell like a spring meadow and a river all at once. He rubs the creams into her beautifully soft but slightly wrinkled skin. They had stayed too long under the water. Tim is patient on the parts of Robyn that the water was particularly hard on. He is determined to restore her to her pre-shower glory, taking the total blame for keeping her under the shower so long.

Eventually satisfied with his handy

work he makes a quick job of moisturizing himself. A few shots of antiperspirant and he is done. Robyn also sprays herself with a mixture of lilies and vanilla. Out of habit, they both find themselves brushing their teeth. They catch each other's eyes in the mirror and smile. A quick rinse and they're done in the bathroom. Tim takes the moisturizer with him as he takes Robyn by the hand and leads her out of the room. They make their way to the last room that needs attention, the master bedroom. They had kept this room for last so that they would not be tempted to fall asleep before they had got to it and finished the process of unpacking. Now they make their way to do just that. Tim also intends to finish the work on Robyn's cunt that he had started in the shower.

The bed is under the large window in the generous bedroom. It's unmade and Tim takes the initiative to dress the large sleeper lightly. A sheet and a light throw is all that is needed given the warm yellow sunshine coming through the light airy drapes. Tim lays Robyn on the bed, on her stomach, encouraging her to just relax. She throws a glance at his cock and is relieved to find that his erection doesn't appear as aggressive now. She wants him to finish what his cock had promised her cunt not too long ago, but she would appreciate a few moments just to catch her breath. He runs his hands over her body all the way from her shoulders down to her feet. He works his fingers into her muscle using the lotion and makes his way back up from her feet and this time ending on the back of her neck. Again, he works his way back down, this time taking brief moments to concentrate on neck, then shoulders, then back, butt, thighs, calves, and feet. His fingers are magical, sending waves of relaxation through her that have her falling in and out of an 'almost' sleep.

Tim take Robyn's feet into his hands, one at a time. He presses down with both thumbs just behind the toes and then runs the pressure up the length of the sole to the heel. He squeezes her heels gently, pressing in deep circles with his thumbs again before fisting his hands and knuckling the entire length of the soles of her feet. Robyn feels like she's just been whisked off to a luxury spa as Tim's expert hands revitalize and rejuvenate her feet. She's completely lost to the massage, not a minute of it wasted as each touch, each tingle, and each squeeze registers within her fully.

Tim's fingers then move up over her calves, each appendage giving its own interpretation of Tim's intention, his palms also joining in on the assault on Robyn's firm calves. Up and down between ankle and knee Tim rubs into the muscle, relaxing it. The cream makes his movements smooth, also adding an alluring shine, a glow to Robyn's already naturally glowing skin. Tim's eyes fall on her ass, and then her pussy, almost hidden in the darkness that is her almost closed legs. He catches glimpses of the entrance to the tunnel he's occupied so many times, and will occupy again before he's done here. He needs to see more.

After a few more cock stiffening glances at where he knows her cunt is Tim finally lets his hands work passed her knees to Robyn's thighs. He rubs up and down the back of them so that his thumbs run through the centre of her legs along her inner thighs. With each upward movement, he digs his thumbs into the darkness, feeling for her pussy. As he rubs back down from ass towards her knees, he gently eases her legs apart. She helps by opening them up slightly. The view of her vagina improves dramatically. He lets his hands run all the way up over her ass and then back down; this time passed her knees to her ankles. As he does this, he places his lips on the delicate ankles, and kisses a path that ends on her pussy, exactly where his tongue wants to be.

He licks her pussy from behind while running his hands delicately now, up the sides of her legs. She raises and lowers her ass, parting her legs a little more to give him more access. He appreciates this allowance and digs his tongue deeper into her cunt. His hands rest on her ass and he parts the firm cheeks just enough to expose her perfect little rosebud. He lets his tongue meander up into the little blooming mound and he runs beautiful circles over it. She raises her butt a little more and he gives her what she wants, a full assault of his tongue on her ass. This drives her wild.

He lingers momentarily inside the tight hole before lifting himself off of it. He kisses her lower back after wetting his middle finger and gently easing it into her ass. This has Robyn gasping, and then panting, begging for more under husky breaths. He lets the entire length of his finger settle inside her, and alternates his kisses on her back with licks across her midsection and bites on her sides. Robyn's ass sways from side to side and then around and around in an attempt to feel every bit of the finger in her. Tim obliges her desire by sending his index finger to meet the middle already digging up a storm inside her. A very loud moan escapes Robyn as she falls facedown into the sheets.

Tim gives her midsection a few bites as he lets his fingers slide out of her a little. Then, as he slides them back inside her, he licks her spine from its base all the way to where it splits to become her shoulders. He has his full weight on top of her now as he sinks his teeth into her shoulder, his fingers still moving in and out of her ass. He kisses and bites her across the broad of her back, kissing the back of her neck and then biting into the soft flesh. He sucks on her as though she tastes like strawberries and takes deep breaths out of her hair as though it smelled of fresh morning coffee.

Settling on her neck for a while, he lets his fingers free themselves from her elated ass and meet quickly underneath her where her pussy awaits, already wet. He finds her clit and allows each finger a solo performance over the moist flower. She straightens her legs and then raises her knees to the sides of her in anticipation of penetration that doesn't come. Tim is milking this moment, and her pussy, for everything they're worth. One by one, his fingers pirouette over her clit, deliberately ignoring her vagina, which spits its desire on any of the fingers that venture too close to it. A few more kisses on her neck, a few more circles on her clit, and then Tim rises to his knees, and gives his handy work a good long look.

He turns her over; whereupon Robyn is met with the largest, firmest erection she's seen on Tim yet. The cock is too inviting for her to resist and she lifts herself up into a sitting position and gives Tim's dripping dick a few sensual licks, followed by an even more sensual series of sucks. She holds the cock and moves it around in her mouth and then over her lips. He watches as she takes it into her mouth and loses as much of it as is possible inside her. Her tongue seems to offer his dick some strong licks while her entire mouth offers some incredible suction. When she can keep herself up no more she releases the cock from her lips and falls back onto the bed.

Tim's lips are immediately on her eyebrows. The gentleness with which he kisses the brows has Robyn close her eyes. This prompts a few kisses on her eyelids. She can't open them even after his lips have lifted off the lids and so Tim plants a few more tender kisses across her forehead, not neglecting her brows and lids as he goes. His gentleness is one of the biggest turn-ons. He has the most amazing ability to switch from Jekyll to Hyde at a whim.

She can't help giggling when he rubs his nose against hers. He lets their noses dance against each other and eventually stops her giggling by planting his mouth on hers. She beats his tongue to it by slipping hers into his mouth before he has a chance to feed her his. He accepts it enthusiastically, almost biting it before sucking gently on it. She teasingly chews on his tongue when she eventually lets him let her have it. The passion that is his mouth soon makes its way to her neck and she again closes her eyes in response to the hot kisses and sucking now happening to her neck.

His mouth finds her breasts and the nipples immediately harden in his mouth. He sucks on them as gently as he would do a meringue crust. She can't help touching herself as his tongue licks her nipples while the breast sits snuggly in his mouth. One hand on her cunt, the other finds the back of Tim's head and she pushes him down onto the breast he's sucking. He takes this to mean that he can suck a little harder, and so he does. She moans as he tugs at the nipple with his teeth. He repeats this on the other breast, and then alternates between them as Robyn fingers herself gently, not too intently, so as not to interfere with the plan she knows Tim has for her pussy.

Her belly gets the attention next, and Tim is deliberate about the warm air he blows over her stomach in-between the kisses he plants on her midriff. She arches upwards as his kisses again become bites, a delicious treat for the normally neglected part of her body. He licks her belly button, both inside it and around it. This unusual sensation has her caught between a giggle and a gasp. His teeth also manage to find her hips, something that totally eliminates the giggles. She gasps loudly and moves from his grip. He follows her, pretends to bite, kissing her instead. She moves into him when she is greeted with lips instead of teeth. Despite the million new sensations, her body has never felt more ready for a fuck.

Tim bites the hand that has rooted itself on her vagina. Immediately Robyn slips the one finger out and lifts it away. Tim graces the pussy with no more than a dozen licks and then starts to lick his way back up towards her face. He fumbles very briefly with the condom but by the time that his mouth is on hers again he's already parting her thighs with his hand and guiding his starship enterprise into her deep space. The curve slips into her smoothly, her cunt having had more than an hour of agonizingly fucktastic foreplay to prepare for it. Tim sends his cock all the way into the back of her cunt on the first stroke, and then he just settles there for a moment so that she can adjust. Content that she has he withdraws to his head and then sends his cock into her harder than before, again all the way to the rear of her cunt. She grabs his firm butt to hold him in place.

Tim uses his cock to stir the juices inside Robyn's vagina for a while, each circle has her tighten the grip on his ass. Round and around his cock moves inside her wet pussy which manages to maintain its signature tightness despite the moisture running down its walls. Tim escapes her grip and brings his cock out to the head again, sending the shaft back into her without warning, one solid pound. In and out of her cunt his cock moves, determined to break through the wall at the end of her tunnel. Deeper and deeper he seems to go, stopping only when she holds him in place whereupon he stirs the shit out of her cunt. There is no denying that Tim is intent on fucking her pussy proper before he lets her sleep. He drills deep into her, his thrusts hard, almost savage. This is exactly the kind of fucking she needs after the incredible foreplay. He knows this. She knows that he does and so she parts her thighs as far as they can go so that Tim can make a solid go of completing the job.

Her vagina no longer tries to hold onto the cock as it slips out of her completely now. Tim has to hold his dick near the base so as not to miss his target for reentry. Completely out he withdraws his log, and then plants the wood inside her in its entirety; out and then fully in, out and fully in his dick moves, forcing Robyn's cunt to climax in stages. There is a sort of ripple effect to her climax as Tim continues this total exit total entry strategy. Eventually her gasps become moans, which become screams and so he sends his dick into her depths full force for the final battle. Half in half out is the new strategy, coupled with wide stirs. Faster and faster he thrusts, harder and harder he pounds her now almost tender pussy with his pecker. She presses down hard on his shoulders as she cums, a river all over the sheets, down her thighs, exciting Tim who continues to thrust long after she has stopped screaming. By the time Tim's screams come and his seed fills the condom inside her, Robyn's vagina is ready to call it a day. They can't move, falling asleep in the midst of the beautiful mess they've just created.

They wake up just as the sun begins to set and make their way, for the first time, to their en-suite bathroom. It has the most delightful tub. They both fit comfortably in it. It isn't long before they've washed the lust off of each other and settle comfortably into the love amidst the bubbles. There's talk of what else might be done to the apartment and chats about what work still remains. But nothing is pressing and so mostly, there is just a satisfied silence. Tim kisses the back of Robyn's neck as she sinks a little lower into the water, between his legs. He holds her tightly and reclines a little so as to make her even more comfortable. Exclusivity definitely had its perks. And Tim and Robyn had just given themselves a solid introduction to every single one!

5 BETTER WHEN BAD!

Prologue

Laura is every bit the wholesome small-town girl. She teaches in middle school, still lives in the apartment above her parent's garage that became her bedroom in high school, and seems to have managed to keep her life free from the complications associated with love and relationships. But *Miss Laura*, as she's fondly known to her seventh graders, has a naughty little secret....

While she walks around the town in plaid and cashmere by day, she dons stilettos and leather by night. Laura is one of only a handful of people in her town who have a mild fascination with BDSM. They've formed a very private, very low-key group, meeting under the guise of a *book club*, where they share fantasies and materials they've come across. It really is nothing more than a casual exchange of ideas and experiences by a group of adults. Occasionally members will meet each other outside of the group for a private show-and-tell.

The restraints on her wrists and ankles are tighter than the cunt between her parted thighs, even with her cunt juice already soaking the linen. Laura appears frozen in a jumping jack, a suspended scissor jump that barely allows for the arch of her back or the slight lift of her groin from the bed. There's nothing to it for her but to sink into the mess of satin and duck feathers underneath her and to brace herself for the solid 8-inch rod dangling above her wet pussy. Her clit beats almost audibly as her masked beau dips his shaft all the way up inside her, drilling her into the bed before he immediately pulls out, the muscles in her pussy struggling in vain to hold on to the pleasure stick. She moans....

"You like that huh? There's some more right here just for you. You want it? Tell me you want it. Better yet, tell *him* where you want it...." Laura's answers to these questions are made in silent moans as the cock slips into her mouth, sliding slowly down her throat as her pussy lifts off the bed, needing the action her mouth is getting. She sucks deep and hard, swallowing the precum filling the back of her throat. Her mouth widens, as suddenly her cunt is stretched open by two, then four fingers, followed almost immediately by the 12-inch ebony dildo she was teased with along with the almost torturous teasing dips of the tool now plowing in and out of her mouth. The toy's 6-inch girth fills her tiny cunt completely. Another series of moans....

She sucks hard on the dick, needing it deep inside her, trying to suck it into her, down into the place where she craves it. The dildo moves around inside her dripping pussy as she pulls on the restraints, desperate to free her hands so that she can help with the violation on her vagina. Laura wants her hands free so that she can grab the firm ass of the Indian accountant in the mask who, along with his beautiful cock, is indulging her need to be sexually dominated. Yes, she likes to dominate, but on nights like tonight, when the whole day has been spent dripping at the thought of being tied down and fucked out of her mind, she needs just that. She relinquishes control and thrusts as high and hard as she can, still not getting the full length of the black rod inside of her. She all but screams....

"What a hungry cunt you have there. You think you can handle it all?" Hemil knows she can't but he really is a fantastic tease. He's coined Laura the ultimate fuck. He doesn't wait for her to answer, slipping another inch of the black cock up her tightening pussy, dipping another inch of his own meat into her mouth. Hemil taps on the base of the dildo, sending stabs of pleasure through her groin up into her breasts. She pulls on the satin knots on her wrists, knowing that she can't undo them, needing to try anyway. He taps again and again, sending wave after wave of pleasure through her tiny body. Then another inch inside her, with effort, her pussy seeming to get smaller the deeper he tries to go. She wants more, but there just isn't space. She moves her waist in circles, trying to ease it in as Hemil moves the tool in countercircles in an effort to create the space needed for at least another inch. She's almost swallowed ten, but the girth is what challenges her pussy, stretching her cunt almost to its limits. She loves it.

Hemil has the arrogance that comes from having ancestors who bear the title of the greatest lovers in the world, which makes him the perfect master for Laura on days when she isn't wielding her whip. He is also very aware of how her body works.

This is due to the fact that they are no strangers to each other, being members of the same *book club*, a secret meeting of conservatives with a fascination for BDSM. Savannah isn't the kind of town where you make public such curiosities, but fortunately, birds of a feather always seem to find each other.

The struggle for a few more inches continues. It's not anguish. It's a beautiful attempt by her cunt to completely understand exactly what nature had in mind when she placed a tunnel riddled with erogenous nerve endings between the outside world and her womb. But her womb is the last thing on her mind as the dildo dances around inside her, a tight squeeze despite Hemil's determination. She exhales, concentrating on relaxing her cunt. The vanity of it all is frustrating. The attempt is an absolute fucking pleasure she suffers gladly.

The *almost* exit of the black rubber made her throw a *don't you dare* look at Hemil. He throws a *try me* look back at her and then pushes the toy back inside her grateful vagina. Still no more than ten inches though, but ten is doing a damn fine job on her pussy all the same. Again, a frustrating exit of six inches, maybe seven inches. The exchange of looks, death stares, another insertion, ten—maybe ten and a half—the repetition enough to draw *white* from somewhere deep inside her pussy.

Hemil suspends his hand so that the dildo is secure. He watches for a few moments as Laura attempts to fuck it. She does a fair job of it too, mind you, the visuals drawing semen through the slit of his own cock. His dick jerks, movements that indicate to Laura and her pussy that they might, just as soon as their current guest has vacated, be getting another visitor. The thought is one that excites both her pussy and madam sufficiently to put a smile on her face.

Laura lets Hemil dildo-fuck her some more. She enjoys that there is just no dick room left inside her and so she can settle into the length inside her comfortably. It's the comfort she feels with Hemil that allows her to allow him to stretch her to her outer and inner limits this way. The long and short of it really is that she just enjoys fucking him, and he obviously enjoys fucking her. His dick seems primed for doing just that if the wet tip is any indication.

With no warning, there is suddenly a void in her cunt where the monster cock just was. The meat in her mouth also extracted just as a stream of hot cum leaves the tip, sticking to her closed lips. Her tongue clears the mess as the black rod finds her mouth, filling it. She bites down on it harder than she would have done if it were real, needing the pressure to keep the monster in her mouth. Hemil needs both his hands now, putting on the sheath that will allow him to take not only himself but also Laura over the edge safely. Her ankles are freed, her knees lifted up towards her breasts, Hemil keeping a firm grip on her ankles.

"Fuck me! Please fuck me...," she breathes the command.

"Oh not yet, little miss. I've got something else for you, you horny little bitch.... Can't neglect your other naughty places...." He teases as well with lips as he does with fingers, slipping two of his thick appendages in his mouth and then sliding them one at a time and then both together into Laura's butthole, so tight he needs to dip his fingers in some of the tiger balm he had used on her inner thighs earlier. Her ass is soon very accommodating. He lets his fingers play long enough for her to need him to fuck her ass, the million stimulated nerves demanding it. She wraps her legs around his waist and almost mounts the throbbing cock herself.

Hemil pulls away briefly. Laura winces as her access to the cock becomes impossible for a distance barely two inches. She needs the rod in her tight butt now, but the cock's owner needs to savor the pleading look on her face, her cunt dripping tiny streams in the direction of the hungry hole. Her waist jerks, involuntarily she thinks, maybe not, needing the power in Hemil's waist to do with his cock what Laura's pleading body knows it is capable of. Another jerk in the general direction of cock...

"I thought I was supposed to be in control here...." Hemil is dragging it out as much as he can, but he's too horny to really keep himself from sticking his purple head into the hungry lubricated hole already primed for swallowing him. He eases his head and then the rest of his shaft into her ass as he leans forward to pull the dildo from her mouth. He pushes it back in as he thrusts, simulating with the dildo in her mouth what his cock is doing to her ass. His thrusts are audible, his pounding savage. She wraps tighter around his waist, her cunt flowing with sticky love pudding as her clit is tickled by the soft curls on his stomach.

His final assault now, he lifts her leg, positioning the lower half of her on her side, positioning himself behind her, her wrists now tied to the same post. No time for her to adjust to this new position. She can't even think about it since she's practically into her orgasm already. His orgasm is close, so he rams her ass again, thrusting the dildo into her soaking slippery cunt, thrusting it deep inside her as he exits her ass, thrusting his cock deep into her butt as he pulls the dildo out, fucking pussy and asshole in tandem. She screams, he screams, her climax reaching its peak but then pausing, along with the dick in her ass and the cock up her cunt. Everything and everyone suspends for a moment—neither to catch their breaths nor to brace themselves, but just for the sole purpose of prolonging the pleasure.

The thrusting resumes. More violent than before, Hemil's cock seems to have grown a few inches, filling her ass almost as completely as the black rod in her pulsating pussy. She needs to cum and so does he. The signs of impending explosions drip in salty beads from both their brows. He digs deeper into her from the front and the back, forcing an almost collision of cocks inside tiny Laura, who practically wraps herself around the cocks inside her, needing them to stay put as every muscle in her pussy pumps surge after surge of pleasure into the hard rubber and the solid muscle in her ass is caught in an almost pleasure vice that it seems to reciprocate.

Wave after wave of absolute pleasure, rivers of heat pushing through every part of her body from his, also from deep inside her into his body, swirling around them, locking them together now to the end.

Hemil rests his cock deep inside Laura. His waist now takes over the work of directing his cock inside her. The muscles and nerves in her pussy are grateful that the hand on the dildo knows not to move, her own cunt working itself into the necessary frenzy for orgasm.

They both fall into a euphoric lull, their minds lost to the lusts engaging every cell in their bodies. The thrusting resumes again, this time measured— and consistent. There is no turning back now. He fucks Laura so deep and so hard that his explosion, having been stopped and started so many times during this fuck session, produces a massive load. There are loud groans as the semen fills the condom so much that it leaks down out of the bottom of it, warming his balls. It takes several hard thrusts to milk him completely, the black dildo soaked in the juices of Laura's deeply satisfied cunt.

"Do this again?" Hemil slaps his limp penis on the sides of her face, Laura enjoying the taste of his freshly showered balls.

"Definitely... And I promise to try to get a handle on my *control issues*," Laura apologizes for fucking the shit out of Hemil's cock even with her hands tied on.

"I forgive you. My dick forgives you. You're a natural dominatrix. You can't help it. But one day you'll let yourself go and allow yourself to be pleasured." He understands the game.

"You do pleasure me."

"You know what I mean, L." He did.

"See you on Tuesday?" They would be attending the weekly meeting at the book club where they would be discussing this experience in abstract.

"Yeah, Tuesday." Hemil shows that he has forgiven her by fucking the shit out of her mouth, then her cunt again in the shower, ending off by massaging her back and washing her hair. In another world, they would have been the perfect couple. In this world, their bodies were well suited to deeply satisfying fucks. No more was needed.

It's never a challenge to get up in the morning because Laura really enjoys her class. Middle school is challenging on its worst days and rewarding on its best. She loves the challenges more than anything else and has a deep fondness for children, the development of whose minds she is charged with. She is doing exactly what she had set out to do with her life, and at 23, she is already deeply satisfied in her career.

But before leaving for school, there is a little ritual that plays itself out before her feet hit the floor, sometimes even before she opens her eyes. Ever since she moved out of the main house in high school and settled in the apartment above the garage, Laura has been able to fully explore her body without the concern of her mother or father barging into her room to kiss her good morning. Now that she is independent, sort of, she can pretty much make as many curious sounds as she likes since the apartment was originally designed as a music room for her rock star-wannabe dad very early in the marriage before the responsibility of Laura came alone. Also, one needed to be let in from the door at the bottom of the side staircase that led into the garage, meaning that she was completely private as long as she remembered to lock the door downstairs. She always did.

The early sound of the morning—the garbage truck, the birds, the dogs down the street—all seems to stir Laura deep inside. These sounds, and the promise of sunrise, send messages to her fingers that there is a warm intimate part of her that needs to be touched. Laura slides her hands under her cotton panties and teases herself along her waistline. Slowly she starts to touch her pussy with her fingers, both hands under the cotton. She doesn't rush the moistening of her cunt, knowing that she has a good two hours before there is any real urgency to get out of bed.

She lets her body produce its own natural lubrication before introducing a finger, then another. She likes the smell of her own cunt and runs the scent past her nose. This gives her a sensory confirmation of her arousal, as do the traces of goo on her fingers. She carefully inserts a finger from each hand and then pulls her pussy open. She pulls as far as she can without causing herself pain and then digs into her wet cunt. Her pants are loud, but there is no need to contain them as the alarm that is her stereo comes on and a morning music program gives the background music.

She digs deeper and deeper into her cunt as her body starts to crave another body, a feeling she knows will pass once the impossibility of this at the moment sinks in. She turns to her side and brings her knees up to her chest as she digs four of her fingers into her pussy, the fingers on the other hand teasing her ass. She loves the double fuck. Her ass is giving and she reaches over into her side drawer after a few moments of self-manipulation, pulls out a slender silver tool, and sticks it completely inside her butt. She turns back onto her back and drops her ass into the bed, sitting on the tool to keep it from moving. This prolongs her orgasm. She learned this early on in her deviant sexual explorations too.

Both her hands again attack her pussy. She pulls harder and digs deeper, grunting like the spoils of a village raid being fucked in turn by a Spartan army. Eight fingers pull her pussy apart and finger up the walls of her cunt. She gyrates so that the silver in her ass moves around. It's only a few minutes of this violation on herself before she is on the edge of orgasm. It feels like hours. She brings it to a symphonic conclusion by practically lifting herself off the bed with the fingers in her cunt and fucking them in the air until her sheets are wet with her satisfaction.

A more delicate stroking takes place in the shower, an almost thank you to her vagina for being so good to her and for being so tolerant. She cleans her pussy carefully, but not after sending delicate whispers with her fingertips over her clit until she has a second orgasm. She has made this double orgasm a ritual since her sexual liberation. That she has the best sex with herself is undoubted....

Tuesdays really are like Mondays, or any other days for that matter—at least for the enthusiastic schoolteacher. Because her life is made up of elements that satisfy her personally, there is never a moment that feels wasted, except maybe moments like this one, with the middle-aged Jonathan North, her school principal, in his office by himself, the school practically empty. Laura is a dominatrix with a secret desire to be dominated, and in her most honest moments, she wants to be dominated by the man with his head in the mound of paperwork on his desk, the man who looks up briefly to smile and wave her off as she says her goodbyes for the afternoon.

In her most secret fantasy, on an afternoon much like this one, *Principal North calls her into his office to discuss something concerning one of her students. He ties her to his chair and....* She quickly brings herself out of the fantasy as she realizes that she's staring. She taps on the wall and then walks off, her thoughts turning to tonight's meeting of BDSM enthusiasts in the entertainment room at Reese Locklear's house. Reese can be thought of as the founding member of the group, having suggested the meetings to become a regular thing after an accidental exchange at his summer lawn party involving whips, cuffs, and a whole lot of sexual envelope pushing.

There is something about like-minded individuals that draws them to each other. Eight people finding each other in a party of over a hundred is a testament to that. Nobody even really remembers the beginnings of the conversation, assumed to have stemmed from a very innocent statement. But before long, there were a few people huddled in a corner, discussing in hushed undertones the mystery that is BDSM. The labeling was strange for some who hadn't before been able to categorize their dark fantasies, and so this became a precursor to follow-up discussions. It's been a regular occurrence for two years now.

Laura can't, even now as she walks up the stairs to Reese's front door, get the image of Jonathan's cock out of her head. Not that she has seen it mind you, but some men just give the most incredibly obvious hints as to what their man meat might look like. Jonathan has a constant bulge in his pants, for example, in perfect alignment with his zipper. This suggests that his limp dick is too large for him to position it to the side of his briefs, so he has to almost tuck it between his legs, creating the perfect bulge formed essentially by the middle of his shaft. Also, occasionally she has, not for lack of looking, caught brief glimpses of his dick head in his inner trouser leg as he walked, indicating that it is a heavy cock that hangs quite low. She wants this cock. More so though, she wants this man to force-feed it to her.

It never takes too long for the meeting to

settle down, everyone eager to get into it. There are seven members present; the eighth standing member, Keenan Brody, is still on his way, needing to pick up the newest member whom he has recruited over a round of golf. The rules are simple when it comes to new recruits. For the safety of the recruit, it is not necessary for a member to disclose whom they would be bringing. After all, once inside the group, having gone through the *initiation*, there is enough leverage either way to make the surprise exciting.

When a member recruits someone, they have to get the person wishing to join the group to make a tape detailing his or her particular fetishes and fantasies. This tape is graphic and authenticated by the member only, whose responsibility it then becomes if the recruit behaves inappropriately or if the privacy of the other members is threatened by the new recruit. It isn't foolproof but the eight members of the group are as careful about their own privacy as they are about the privacy and protection of each other. And since they all have no desire to lose the intimate setting where they can indulge their inner animals, they guard the group well.

Apart from Reese, Laura, Keenan, and Hemil, the other four members are Luther, Stacey, Lyn, and Selwyn, a mix of professionals in their 30s and 40s. Everyone has a specific area of interest, and they all try, through research outside of the group, to expand each other's knowledge of these areas and to enrich each individual's experiences. Occasionally they partner up outside of the group to offer more hands-on assistance. Hemil and Laura are the most *hands-on* with each other though, but nobody ever really knows who's been with whom, just to avoid unnecessary attachment issues.

Stacey is a 35-year-old nurse with a thing for mild pain and multiple cocks. She likes her pussy stretched. You wouldn't think it looking at her, a five-foot beauty with a bit of flesh on her body, giving her perfectly positioned curves. She looks like a nerdy teenager, the babysitting kind with no social life and a sexy minx hidden beneath her black-rimmed spectacles. But when it comes to sex, she is far from nerdy, or innocent, or delicate, or any of the other things her appearance would have you believe. She likes it rough, very rough, enjoying having her boundaries pushed. Stacey wastes no time in sharing her weekend escapade with the group, everyone closing their eyes so that the story plays out like a film in the collective cinema of their minds.

*The safe word was "**peanut**." Everybody had*

already received the text with the word that would bring the proceedings to an immediate halt should anybody suddenly be uncomfortable with the course of events, anybody being Stacey of course since it was her pussy on the line. Stacey would be playing with Alessandro, a nursing student. They would be joined by Pedro and Louis, cousins from Colombia who worked in hospital maintenance. They had met online a few weeks prior, and after an initial tentative briefing over coffee at the cousin's downtown apartment, they all decided that they were comfortable enough with each other to give it a go. There were no real rules, no commitments, just the safe word as a control. Other than that, there were no holds barred. The men enjoyed group sex and didn't mind indulging Stacey's need for a bit of pain since they too were turned on by the one-cunt-many-cocks dynamic.

Alessandro always brought the toys, his backpack the safest carrier since it would be tucked safely in his locker. He was also a student so it wasn't at all unexpected that he would walk around with one. Pedro and Louis usually just came with Colombian cock and enthusiasm. They also brought with them the ability to follow Alessandro's instructions, despite him being ten years short of their thirty. The American born to Greek immigrants always insisted on a dick powwow before their assault on Stacey, knowing that the chances of finding another bitch so willing to be brutalized by a group of pussy-hungry savages would be zero to none in Savannah. So they needed to make sure that she always got what she wanted.

Stacey was indeed a rare find in a town where every pussy had its pick of at least fifteen pricks.

Tonight was simple enough: a few clamps and a couple of sets of Thai balls that ranged in size from small to no-fucking-way. Surgical gloves were standard. There was cord to tie her up and enough condoms for each of the dicks to go around more than once if they were up to it. They usually were. There was no speaking once the venue was entered, this adding to the tension, increasing the focus on the fucking, and also making sure that the safe word would stand out.

Stacey was first to arrive, the blindfold on the small table in the boiler room being self-explanatory. In the dark there would be no faces, no names, and no voices; there would just be three hard cocks and one quivering pussy. She doesn't wait for anything that indicates that the others are here, or on their way, donning the blindfold, standing in the dark, getting more and more uncomfortable. The edge drives the adrenalin, which in turn fuels her sex drive. The minutes feel like hours, the mounting tension moistening the inside of her cotton panties.

Her hair is pulled back hard, her assailant breathing into her ear as he puts his hand into her scrubs and palms her pussy over the cotton, pushing her back against his cock, already erect. He's already naked. Her breasts are cupped by a second pair of hands, her top unbuttoned as her lips are bitten, the unshaven face of this second man rubbing against the side of her face, nibbling her ear, filling it with his tongue. He's naked too, his hairy chest rubbing against her breasts, now fully exposed with her top on the floor.

Stacey knows there should be a third man as per the arrangement. It doesn't even matter who is missing, just as long as he shows up. She's braced for serious fucking, and two dicks just won't do when your pussy has prepped for three. Her pants are off, then her panties, pussy, and ass now sandwiched between two hard cocks. This mild play is predictable and, for the most part, boring for Stacey, but she starts to ooze pussy saliva, knowing that this is just her predators' way of lulling her into complacency so that the moment of full-on cunt savagery takes her by surprise, maximizing its effect.

Her legs are lifted off the ground and she is carried to the table, wide enough for her to sit but not to lie down. The steel surface sends literal shivers up her spine, her back against the wall. Her legs are spread, her feet placed flat on the table. She's sitting with her pussy exposed, the slit aching in anticipation.

Her pussy lips are parted violently, pulled forward, then apart. Her examiner shoots some saliva on her cunt and then sticks a gloved finger deep inside her. She can't move back away from him, another finger making a grand entrance. There's no warming her up as her cunt is invaded by five slithering fingers, the entire gloved fist up inside her, making her gasp. Briefly, the metal clamps on her nipples distract her from her cunt, but only briefly. She wasn't ready for the finger, not moist enough for a cock let alone a whole hand. But pushed up against the wall, she has no choice but to take it. She almost rocks in an attempt to calm herself, finding the sides of the table, grabbing on.

The sound of the balls excites her; she knows this pleasure. The balls are forced in their order of elevation up into her pussy as soon as the fist eases out. This insertion is almost impossible in her sitting position despite her fuck hole having just been ripped open by a fist, but the hands doing it are determined. There's barely enough time for her to fully register when the no-fucking-way ball closes off her cunt with another fist-sized seal. Her mouth is empty but again she gags. It feels like the balls are going to come out of her mouth. She needs to straighten out, feeling stuffed. Her knees are held in place by strong hands as her clit receives a series of rapid licks, the hard vibration forcing her vagina to squeeze tightly around the balls that now push the walls of her cunt out in a pyramid. It starts to feel like the balls are in her stomach, but she reminds herself that this isn't possible. Then the clamps, this time harder on her nipples, restrict the blood flow to the sensitive mounds. A mouth pulls on the metal chains dangling from the clamps and her nipples redden with pain. She exhales hard.

The table is mounted by a third man, large if his thick legs are any indication. Stacey makes space for his feet on the table by holding on to his legs. This man braces himself against the wall and drops his cock into range of Stacey's face. Her mouth opens up to receive it, taking it in one continuous movement until she throws her head back and tries to wriggle the cock out of her mouth, her head flailing side to side. It's too much too soon. She's offered four inches of relief and shows her appreciation by hungrily sucking on the length of cock left inside her wet mouth.

Suddenly she's alone on the table again. She's pulled away from the wall along with the table and turned over so that her stomach alone is on the table, her feet on the ground—two cocks in her mouth, a tag team. The balls slip one by one out of her, the extraction slow and deliberate. Her hands are tied behind her back, the cord then pulled down so that her ankles are tied by the same cord to the legs of the table, her pussy hanging over the edge, her ass open to invasion from above.

She's pulled up to standing position just as a dick rams her asshole, ripping into the un-lubed passage. Quick thrusts quickly coat the entrance mercifully with some of the lube from the condom. The cock in her ass is unrelenting, fucking her so that if it wasn't for the table, or the man now sitting on the table, his legs between hers so that his cock holds her up, she might have fallen over. Both her holes are packed, pounded deep. Her face is pulled forward so that a cock is again stuffed into her by a man who can only be standing on the table, more accurately squatting on the table. Her mind admires the acrobatics of it all.

Stacey knows that her climax won't come in this position, too much going on in the way of pleasure. She also knows though that she won't be disappointed. The three men rotate her holes, each of them climaxing only one cock finds ass. She is still some ways off from her own climax, but now that their own loads have been shot, the focus is on her. Everyone knows that the sight of Stacey's orgasm inspires every cock in the room to an encore.

Stacey is pulled up again, untied, the table pushed aside—legs apart, her clit bitten on, and her pussy licked, sucked, and tongue-fucked by three mouths, her legs held down by many hands. She's dripping but it's no climax. Pulled down to the ground, each leg taken in hand by one of the men, the third in charge of her pussy, again her fuck hole is exposed. Her legs are pulled apart as far as they will go, the balls again descending into her with even no-fucking-way making it all the way inside her cunt. With the balls inside her, her legs are lifted so that a cock can find her ass. She splits as the dick fills her, its owner pushing her legs down over her head. Again, it's her ass that milks all three cocks.

Time to milk Stacey....

The balls are pulled from her, exposing her pussy completely. She stays on her back, the cold concrete providing a contrast between fucking hot and fucking cold. Fingers pull on her full lips, her cunt wanting attention but getting none. The pulls on her clit are hard, the pain incredibly beautiful. Thirty fingers are definitely better than ten are, and all thirty make light work of her cunt and ass. She can't move with a cock in her mouth, her head held in place by knees on either side. The other two men all but lay on her parted legs, knees raised. She's pinned down, with all three men having access to her cunt. They work it rigorously with their fingers until her cunt moistens sufficiently for even the largest of the fists to make a full entrance. Fist after fist slides in and out of her gaping pussy, which contracts and expands with the elasticity of experienced expert cunt. Needless to say, nobody shouts **peanut***, Stacy all but convulsing as she cums all over the last pussy-pounding puncher to slide out of her.*

The doorbell brings the group from the theater in their heads just as Stacey exhales hard through her mouth and the last of the hands is pulled from her cunt. Everybody opens their eyes just as Keenan walks in, followed immediately by his recruit.

"Started without us, I see…Laura, you should know Jonathan right? Everybody… Jonathan North!" Keenan cheekily smiles.

Laura gasps….

Acting awkward around Jonathan would be childish, so Laura keeps her head and makes no signs that would give away her extracurricular activities shared with the headmaster. For the most part, nothing really changes between them professionally, but Laura does find herself entertaining her fantasies about the man a little more, this probably due to the new access she has to him.

She catches him in a moment where he

thinks nobody is looking and he adjusts his penis. In fact, if she wasn't staring at his hand on his crotch under his desk, she wouldn't have noticed. She taps on his wall again and waves a goodbye; he uses his dick hand to wave back. She lets the thought of his cock enter her mind completely now and walks quickly to her car. Laura is far too imaginative to let the suggestion of Jonathan's dick pass her by, and so she rushes home to entertain this thought....

In the confines of her bedroom, she lets the cock touch the inside of her thigh and dig without warning or preparation into her cunt. Her fingers simulate what her mind has her to believe it would be like. More determined than she usually is, she doesn't wait for natural lubrication. She doesn't want any lubrication as she imagines Jonathan North taking her pussy without her permission and making it do whatever his dick needs it to do.

Laura ravages her dry pussy for less than a minute before it starts to pulsate and the line between fantasy and reality is crossed. She closes her eyes and fucks herself as rough and hard as she imagines Jonathan will. She rides her hand and muffles the sound of her pleasure by burying her face in her pillows. Laura turns herself over several times in her bed before eventually she cums, left to face the reality that the wet cunt between her legs has been left wanting by her hand. She has now become obsessed with being fucked by Jonathan. But that there is a possibility that it might happen is a mystery for a while yet until one day....

They soon discover, to her delight, that Jonathan isn't as much of a dark horse as had been thought by all, including Miss Laura, who learns that he's actually quite a cheeky bugger—a very adventurous one too. His naughty streak starts to uncover itself as the days pass, but only after his third visit to the book club does he allow the veil to come off completely. He chooses to take a shot at storytelling, and before anybody else can take the first spot, Jonathan introduces himself officially to the group by telling them of his first escapade on the *dark side*.

Jonathan is too beautiful for a man for the girls to close their eyes as he speaks, the men watching him out of courtesy, this being his first time to speak and all.... Jonathan's voice is as deep as his eyes are dark. His southern drawl makes the story instantly intriguing.... Before he starts the story though, he does something that nobody in the group has dared do before. It is a line that, until Jonathan crossed it, nobody even knew it existed. Jonathan takes each of the women's hands and runs them down the length of his penis over his pants. The men laugh at this, envious and not. The women, including Laura, register intrigue.

He then takes his preparation for his tale a little further and unzips his trousers, pulling out his large dick and letting it hang out in front of him. Everybody registers a puzzled expression, Keenan asking his friend if he was drunk. Confirming that he wasn't, Jonathan proceeds to explain that with a dick like his, large by most standards but not the largest cock in the world, you needed to have a "sense" of it if you were to understand the true essence of his sexcapades and if the impact of what it meant to his partners was to have any resonance.

There is a measure of concurrence as Jonathan returns his whip and everyone nods in mock understanding. The men are sure he was just showing off; the women are glad that he did. Now there was no doubt in anyone's mind that following the visuals, every woman in the room would fall over herself in an attempt to be the vixen in the tale that was to follow. Jonathan tells his story....

I had met her during a conference in Atlanta. Her name was Jane. She was tall, leggy, a secretary. Red hair tied in a high bun, out of her face, made her attractive but unattainable, as high buns are known to do. We had spoken briefly during lunch and were going to drive to the hotel we were both staying at together in my rental. The second half of the conference went on forever, my mind on her full lips, her perfect teeth, and her tongue. She didn't keep me waiting, thankfully.

Once in the car I drove around for a while, making idle conversation, trying to get a feel for her. There were more awkward silences than chats as my thoughts fed blood to my cock, her eyes catching the expansion. I made sure first that we were close enough to the hotel for her to make a comfortable escape if my bulge offended her in anyway, but the smile on her face let me know that she was impressed. I drove on, joining rush-hour traffic with no real direction, destination climax.

After three traffic lights of silence, I figured "what the fuck" and unzipped. The worst thing that could happen was that she would get out and take a cab back and I would have to beat my own meat. So I threw caution to the wind, whipped out the old boy, and watched her eyes as my dick dropped onto my thigh in her direction. No turning back, I grabbed her secretary bun and pushed her head onto my cock just as the red light went green, my dick slithering into her hot mouth, her fleshy lips wrapping tightly around my shaft.

Her throat was impressive as she swallowed more of me than I can recall anybody else ever doing. There was no choking as I guided her head up, then down, up, and then further down, in the middle of downtown Atlanta traffic. Her teeth bit gently into my dick, releasing just before I screamed, soothing the bites with her warm, slippery tongue. I managed a deeper thrust every time I brought the car to a complete halt.

I knew my dick excited her because it wasn't long before she was touching herself, moaning loudly, loud enough for me to turn up the radio, just in case. I looked around at the other cars, paranoia making me think they were all looking at me, this assumption hardening my cock even more. My stiffening cock soon had my accomplice fingering herself. It was time to up the ante....

She bit my cock some more, the bites sending shots of pleasure into my thighs, blood growing my meat even more. Her tiny fingers struggled briefly with my belt, needing it undone for her own reasons—reasons that made my underwear unnecessary. It was the kind of underwear that allowed for a flash escape of cock in an emergency, but she wanted pants down. I obliged. With a mouth like hers, how could I not. Her fingers sent the kind of urges through my penis that just made me wanna fuck the hell out of her mouth and let everyone around me know exactly what I was doin'.

She needed minimal coaching, taking more of my dick in her mouth every time I touched the back of her head. She lathered my balls in her saliva and then traced her wet fingers along her clit, which must have been achin' because she started to pull on her panties, unable to remove them in her current position. It was time for that filly to be mounted, but I had a bit of a twist in store for her.

I made a turn into a quieter road, pulled my pants down to my ankles, and instructed her to free her pussy and to then perch her moist cunt on my dick so that she could ride the shit out of it while driving us back to the hotel! She was on my cock in two shakes, riding my dick before the car started moving. I slowed her down, reclined my seat completely so that I was invisible to the outside world, got her to driving, and then slowly, gently, deeply fucked her little cunt until her knuckles turned white on the steering wheel. It took everything in me not to sit up and see what the drivers around us were making of her wild dancing.

We pulled into the basement parking and found a corner spot where I turned her over and fucked her face down for good measure. Neither of us looked too worse for the wear when we walked through the lobby and made our way to the safety of our rooms for a much-needed shower. I never did see her again. But I sure as hell never forgot that sweet pussy and the adventurous dame it was attached to....

So he was into adventurous public sex. Go figure. Laura was surprised. She was also deeply aroused by his southern accent describing the abilities she had already assured herself he had. She loved hearing him say the word *pussy*; and she liked his references to his cock, the way he seemed to confirm that it was his and that he would do with it whatever the fuck he pleased. She wanted his cock now more than ever....

She played the story back over and over in her head once she had got into bed. One phrase kept creeping up on her: *she swallowed more of me than I can recall anybody else ever doing.* Was he hinting, taunting, or daring her? Was this a challenge directed at her and to her tiny cunt that could manage Hemil comfortably but strained under the invasion of their 12-inch playmate? It would definitely be like sleeping with Goliath, Jonathan being an impressive man in stature and his cock being unusually large, at least for Laura. She made a mental note to accept the challenge, confirming this acceptance by running her fingers into her moist cunt and stroking herself to sleep....

The best way for her to prepare herself for the challenge that was Jonathan was for her to solicit the help of good old dependable Hemil. She couldn't let him know of course that her new determination to take in the entire 12 inches was fueled by her fantasy about Jonathan and by the challenge he hadn't even formally made, her mind needing her to have heard the taunts hidden in his story. She knew that if she just told Hemil, it might bruise him sufficiently for him to never want to fuck her again. She couldn't risk that. So she figured the best way to force him into helping her would be in her trusted whips and chains.

The leather cat suit covers the entire surface of her body, exposing only nipples, ass, and cunt. The 6-inch stilettos give her a perfect *fuck-me-standing* posture. Demure schoolteacher Laura has transformed into Hemil's cock's favorite tease, her whip tracing the length of his pulsating pecker as he sits with his hands cuffed behind his back. Hemil's industrial penthouse is perfect for these escapades, providing the perfect fuck pad, high enough off the ground to be private even with all the curtains open. His cock is now begging to be touched, dripping warm jizz, his balls expanding and contracting with every crack of the whip at his side.

Laura wraps the leather cords around his neck, squeezing. He fucks the air, trying to breathe through his cock. She releases, pulling his head back hard enough and far enough for her pussy to sit on his face. The position is uncomfortable at best, his neck taking strain, his head lifting involuntarily, invariably pushing his nose and mouth into her cunt. She tightens the grip and Hemil all but bites into her perfect pussy. The tighter she chokes, the harder he sucks, seemingly extracting oxygen from inside her along with liquid traces of arousal. She teases him like this, satisfying herself with his mouth.

Hemil thrusts violently in the air, his

cock needing a tight, hot place. She rewards this gyration with crack after crack of her whip on his thighs, his mouth alternating between screams and pussy licking. She drags the three cords up between his legs over his balls and up around his cock before whipping him again. His dick snakes and then jerks to the side as the leather kisses it. The painful lashes on his legs are voided by the pleasure this offers to his cock.

She teases him like this until he starts to trickle cum through the tip of his rock-hard wood. She un-cuffs him and hands him the dildo, taunting him to avenge himself. She all but orders him to feed it to her as she stands astride over him, both her hands on his cock. Instead, he pulls her down onto his own cock, needing a few seconds of relief. After a couple of solid thrusts, he lets her stand. Standing again, she receives six unexpected inches. She staggers forward, the remaining six inches of the black rod inside her dangling outside her cunt. She grips the base of the shaft just as it starts to slip out.

Hemil is already behind her, his hand on the cock. He pulls her back towards him, steadying her, feeding her a few more inches. Laura indicates for the bed and Hemil obliges. She knows, as does he, that there is no way she can take the full length of the toy standing. She's never managed it comfortably lying down. But she's on a mission tonight. She will learn to take it all in effortlessly. She has to if she is going to impress Jonathan.

He carries her to his bed, her legs crossed so as not to lose the progress already made. On her back, the whip wrapped around Hemil's neck again, the reigns in her hands, she pulls him towards her, spreads her legs, and instructs her Indian slave to feed her. When he hesitates, she tightens her grip, Hemil plunging more black into her. Laura chokes him harder with the whip, then harder still. He realizes that the only way to avoid being strangled is to ram the entire rod into her. And so he does....

It works, Laura taking her hands off the whip and grabbing Hemil's forearm. He smiles to himself, remembering their last session where Laura flipped the script and didn't allow him to dominate as planned. He decides to exact some delicious revenge, forcing her hands off his and leaning onto her so that his abdomen keeps the dildo in place, his face on Laura's. He bites her lip and slides his dick into her unprepared ass. She has no choice but to take it.

Hemil's dick is deep inside her, thrusting slow circles in her tight ass. Her cunt is focused on its own intruder, unable however to make any significant moves. Laura relaxes and accepts the assault. She contracts the muscles of her pussy, squeezing tight around the dildo, trying to ascertain the maximum threshold so that she knows most of the discomfort that she could feel. Of course, she knows that the girth of the pussy pounder is an unrealistic exaggeration designed by sadomasochists, and so she relaxes in the knowledge that somewhere deep inside her is enough cunt room for all of Jonathan's cock.

Just to be sure, she pushes her cunt against Hemil as he continues his ass fucking. If she can feel the bones in the sides of his waist, then she figures that his stomach has successfully pushed the 12 inches inside her completely. She isn't at all surprised that she has managed this, knowing that there is nothing that cannot be achieved with the correct motivation. And with her carrot dangling clearly in front of her, she was going to do what is needed to ensure that she would soon be done by Mr. North.

Laura needs to cum but doesn't want the dildo to do it. So as soon as Hemil starts his signature uniform thrusting, she places her hands on his chest and tells him to wait. He looks at her questioningly, continuing his thrusting. She repeats the instruction, throwing him enough to break the rhythm. Frustrated, he pulls out to check if she's okay. She's fine. In fact, she's more than fine as she slowly pulls the dildo out and instructs him to suit up. He does without taking his eyes off the pussy even once, which releases its prisoner and then seals its entrance as though it had never been opened.

Grabbing her legs, he pulls her towards the edge of the bed and onto his cock. From the added leverage he has in his almost standing position, supported by the floor and yet not, he manages maximum penetration. This is exactly what she needs, her cunt slippery from its recent exertion. He doesn't mind, using his foot support to carry himself, balancing himself as he assaults her pussy from a precarious height at even more daring angles. His rise is brief, his fall and subsequent drilling deep as he deliberately loses his balance. She knows this won't be quick, his dick needing to adjust to the sensation before it can even begin to comprehend a finish line. She settles into the next thirty minutes of super-fucking before finally surrendering, along with Hemil, to the inevitable... another series of deeply satisfying orgasms.

Back at her own house, she is surprised to find that she is no longer thinking of Jonathan. Well not really. Her thoughts have shifted to herself and her desire for dominance; she knows that she herself enjoys dominating. Surely, it was too early for her to be having a sexual change of heart. Was she already going through the dreaded "I want to settle down into a normal relationship where I belong to a man and he tells me what to do" phase? She hoped not.

Remembering the first time she dominated a man, back in college, she questions this behavior for the first time. Was it that her own "first time," in Bradley Haynes's bedroom when she was 17, was all about him? Was it this that made her decide to make all subsequent experiences about her? If so, what was it now that made her want to be fucked ala Bradley?

He kissed her long, she remembers, and that resulted in her pussy moistening. But she didn't know what to expect and didn't even look at his dick, only feeling it fumble for entry into her vagina. Her resistance irritated him and so eventually, she just put her own hand on her own mouth and relaxed her thighs, at which point the hard teenage cock abruptly found its way inside her for the first time.

There was no kissing after that point, his interest seemingly captured by something on the wall behind her head. His thrusts were slow and boring, even for her virginal self. In fact, the pain dulled so quickly she had hoped that the pleasure would make up for the initial discomfort. He was contorting his face and fumbling to get his dick out of the condom just as she started to feel the sensations of fucking. Needless to say, it was not as good for her as it was for him.

So when Laura got to college, no longer precious about her pussy, she took the college boys by storm, enjoying the seniors with their experienced dicks, ensuring a fuck that lasted longer than a standard commercial. And all through college, up until recently, she has been having super-charged orgasms as a result of her dominatrix alter ego. But things were changing up a bit. They had done so since she first realized her attraction towards North.

That was it then. She needed to get the old man out of her system. That would at least confirm for her either way what the discrepancy between body and mind actually was. She started to ponder the details of this meeting. How would they ever be alone in a public place? Would he consider a private meeting? She knew that in her fantasies, he fucked her in his office. But knowing what she did about him, this seemed unlikely.

Whatever the circumstance would be, it needed to happen soon. The frustration was bordering on unbearable. Laura pulls her panties off and turns off her bedside lamp. She deliberately thinks of Jonathan now as she uses her fingers to extract lubrication from her cunt. She takes out the 12 inches she "borrowed" after the session with Hemil earlier and just confirms that she had successfully graduated to full length.

She hadn't been able to cum with this tool earlier and so she tries for this feat now. In the dark, her mind can take her wherever she wants to go and she goes straight to North's office, the dick morphing to his. She pushes hard so that it makes its way inside her. She sits up and then on it in order to get it all in. The base is all she has to handle with and so she grips the end of it and works her pussy well. The resulting climax surprises her. It is more complete than even the one she had earlier with Hemil.

The exercise is repeated a few times before she eventually falls asleep. She wakes up not only refreshed but also rejuvenated. She takes her time in the shower, removing the stray hairs on her legs and cunt. She picks out a knee-length skirt and cotton blouse, deliberately avoiding the underwear drawer. She checks herself in the mirror, taking in her own scent—vanilla and jasmine. She looks and smells good enough to eat. It is her intention to be eaten.

Laura takes a moment to look at herself

in the mirror. A good few hours left before the school bell will ring, she decides to take her prepared self for a test drive. She undresses carefully again and examines her legs. She's done an excellent job of shaving. She checks her pussy, clean and smooth. Again, her workmanship is impeccable. She gets the dildo, which she had already cleaned for its return to its owner. She soaks it in hot water to prepare the tool and gets some lube in her bathroom cupboard.

On her bed, she fingers the lube, a cherry-scented gel, but then wipes it off her fingers. She decides to see just what the full ramification of a quick stolen moment in Jonathan's office would be. She anticipates discomfort. But if she knows the extent of this discomfort, she can probably fake her way through it. She parts her legs and positions the dildo over her lips. She runs it briefly over her clit and then finds the entrance to her pussy. She brings her knees up on either side of her and looks away as she forces the warm rubber into her cunt. She's underestimated her thrust and gasps as seven inches immediately fill her up.

Instead of pulling out, Laura looks away again, her face finding the pillow, and rams the remaining five inches into herself. She can't convince herself that it isn't painful, and so she slowly pulls it out, not all the way but just to allude to relief. She rams it into her pussy again before she loses her nerve and then pulls out again for the purpose of illusion. Determination on her face, she pictures Jonathan, not inside of her but as the hand on the dildo. She rams the rubber intruder all the way inside of herself as she talks to herself, imagining he might dare her to take the fucking cock and tell her to be a good little bitch and take it.

Again and again, the dildo finds the very back of her pussy—the very depths of her discovered. She loses herself to it, thrusting now with a hand and a strength not her own. Her own face hides from the violation as though she was no part of it. Jonathan is the one stretching her cunt. Her reward will be his hot live cock inside of her, if she can just suffer this little intruder. She needs to have a well-behaved cunt for the prime prick that is Jonathan's. Nothing less will do. She can't afford not to please him, knowing that pleasing him essentially is pleasing herself.

Laura is surprised when she finally opens her eyes. She is on her knees with the dildo still in her cunt. Her hands cupped between her legs hold it there. She is absolutely soaked in cunt juice and has no recollection of the point of orgasm. All she knows is that she feels as though she has just had the most satisfying sex of her life. She feels, unlike the other masturbatory rituals, as though she has actually had another presence in the room. If nothing else this confirms the absolute necessity for her to do what she must to get the dick that has become her obsession inside of her.

Even if Jonathan hadn't intended the challenge, she had accepted it. And since she had accepted it, it was official. She would make a fool of herself today if she had to, but by the time she got home from work today, she will have had Jonathan North's dick inside of her or be fired for sexually harassing the principal. If only her personality was as docile as she appeared. But no, she just couldn't walk away from a challenge, even a perceived one. She also needed to set her own mind at rest and figure out once and for all if she was obsessed with North or if she was over her dominatrix phase and was ready to move on to a real relationship.

It was during the first interval that Laura found an appropriate moment to whisper in Jonathan's ear, as he exited the staff bathroom, that she wasn't wearing any panties. Intentionally, she walks off before he can respond. This thought is left with him for the rest of the day. She also finds many reasons to see North's secretary, knowing that this means that he will catch glimpses of her in his window as she bent over the secretary's desk. This is all that is needed to lay the groundwork.

Laura has barely finished her class when North's secretary, on her way home after being dismissed early, sticks her head in the classroom. "North says Randal Willard's folks have confirmed that they can come by this afternoon. The meeting will be in his office at 3." There is no meeting of course and Laura wets herself at the thought that her catch has been hooked.

She walks into his office just before 3. The administrative building is deserted except for the janitor. *This is the audience needed for Jonathan's arousal* she assumes. Her assumption is correct. Jonathan instructs her to sit on the seat closest to his at the small boardroom table in the office. He doesn't ask for her permission to confirm her whisperings from earlier. His hands are greeted by a willing shaven pussy waiting for penetration.

The door is not locked, the janitor's whistles not too far off, getting louder and louder. Jonathan gets up and pulls Laura up with him. He moves her to the filing cabinets in the corner and motions her between them. He lifts her skirt up over her waist and admires her ass, running his fingers through her crack all the way to her cunt. She winces.

"Shhh!" he instructs. The janitor is busy in the secretary's station.

Jonathan's dick doesn't disappoint. Laura can't see it with her back to her principal. He wets the tip of his dick with his own saliva and forces his soft head into her dry hole. She gasps. He pushes more of his thick limp penis inside her, forcing her up against the wall and on to her tiptoes. This isn't how she had imagined it. In her head, there were cuffs, or at least a rope, and the desk. She should be tied to his desk. But no, here she was, her breasts against the dry wall in the principal's office, fully clothed, the principal with just his dick out of his zipper, not even erect but making its spongy way inside her. The dick creeps up inside her, hardening as it goes, filling her, exciting her now, but still, this wasn't the fantasy.

Laura feels for Jonathan's pants. They're still on. Is this just a quickie, the moment not only too tempting to pass up but also not sufficient to indulge anything more than good old friction and climax? He grabs her shoulders and braces her against the wall as his cock becomes fully erect inside her. Jonathan goes onto his knees a little as his dick reaches full length. He's not too sure if Laura can take his 12 inches. This is why he enters her soft. He needs to be sure not to do too much damage too quickly. His thrusts are slow and deliberate, forcing moisture from the places deep inside her cunt that manufacture the love potion that makes fucking fantastic. The white on his cock is the cue Jonathan has been waiting for. She's ready!

He gives a few more gentle thrusts before forcing his cock all the way up inside her without warning. He drills her tiny cunt so deep and so hard that he lifts her off the ground, he himself now standing up straight. He pushes his arms under her arms so that his hands are above her head against the wall and her arms hold on to his arms, her hands reaching for his, not getting close for his height. He has literally impaled her with his solid cock and hung her over his arms so that if he lowered his arms, she would fall onto his cock with no way of escaping the rod. With her feet off the ground, she is totally at his mercy now, the need for any other sort of restraint completely void. Laura finds herself well and truly between a cock and a hard place.

North pushes her against the wall, into it. He lifts her higher before dropping her onto his cock a little. He lowers himself to give her pussy some relief, briefly, before standing up straight, impaling her again. She tries to climb up his arms, the sweat on both of them making it impossible; she just slips back down onto the rock-hard dick with nowhere to run. Her legs offer no support, her feet unable to find the ground. All sensation is concentrated in the tiny area that is her flowering pussy. She has no way of controlling any aspect of what is happening to her. Everything about the situation is wrong. She hates it, wanting to scream for him to stop. But her pussy screams for him to continue, grateful. The janitor also makes screaming impossible.

"That's twelve inches right there, Ma'am," he says this in her ear just after he licks the side of her body with his thick hot tongue. He tries for her nipple, only getting the side of her breast. It's enough to heighten his arousal, adding to his girth a little, pleasing her and him. So this is what 12 inches felt like. She makes a mental note to thank Hemil for what was now possible.

Laura cannot contain her screams. She can't control her breathing. She can't control a damn thing as Principal North fucks her up the wall with the force of a hundred devils. His cock breaks every barrier she thought she had and shoots shard after fiery shard of white-hot fuck fury deep inside her fuck hole, now tender for the absolute violation. She needs no other part of herself touched now with every nerve, every muscle, and every pleasure center in her body having traversed the length and breadth of her and set up base camp inside her cunt. He holds a sweaty palm over her mouth and then lets go. She knows to be quiet, the janitor emptying North's bin.

North drops his arms to his side and lets the full measure of his manhood settle deep inside the pussy wrapped around it. There is nothing now for Laura to grab on to, and so she all but sits on North's cock. His strong legs keep them both up as he fucks her hard, mercilessly sticking her into the wall, she holding onto the vertical, pushing herself down onto the cock. Her wet pussy drips onto her thighs and is wet enough now for her to be thrilled with the mammoth fucker inside her. Jonathan's arms are under hers again, him standing straight again, and again Laura is impaled.

He continues this as the janitor cleans, fucking her harder as the vacuum buzzes become alive. There is no way the man cleaning the room doesn't know that there are people in here fucking. The smell is unmistakable. But he just carries on with his work, not once coming close to the filing cabinets in the corner. This was too close for comfort, too close for sheer luck. Did he know that they were there? In all likelihood, he did. Laura accepted this and already moved on in her head. This impaling was worth any side looks she might receive from the janitor in the hallways.

The door closes and Jonathan pulls away from the wall so that Laura falls forward. He thrusts as she walks forward on her hands trying to get a grip. She resembles a wheelbarrow, Jonathan being the gardener. He lifts her towards him and then high enough into the air for his dick to leave her cunt. He needs to see what her arse is made of. She stiffens at the realization of his intention. She hadn't prepped her ass for 12 inches. She would never be able to take his massive cock in her tiny ass. With one thrust, Jonathan proves her wrong.

He goes limp briefly, her tight ass cutting off circulation to his cock. But as she realizes that he's already inside, she starts to relax, giving him a range of motion that allows for friction and a mammoth re-erection. She's against the wall again, holding herself up as he fucks her hard into the wall from behind. Her ass is accommodating, but just barely. He has to lift her up onto the wall for a full-length thrust. It takes an hour of these aided thrusts for her to eventually relent to full-on ass fucking all the way up inside her. North appreciates this.

He's careful not to shoot his load inside her, pulling out only after he's opened the condom. He puts it on quickly so as not to lose momentum and then thrusts his armored warrior in her cunt. She closes her eyes, knowing that there will be no contact, save for pussy and prick. He fucks her with all the gusto he can muster in the absence of an audience and brings her to a thrilling climax. She falls on the floor in a breathless heap. He bends over and brushes the side of her face.

"Everything I thought you would be."

"Thanks, I think...."

"No Laura, thank you."

Laura reaches her epiphany along with her fourth orgasm, Jonathan enjoying his handiwork, taking in the look on Miss Laura's face. She can't possibly take more pleasure, but Jonathan seems to have an unlimited cum reserve. Her own juices have all but run dry, the bulk of her flow on her thighs. Jonathan carefully cleans her up, helping her gather herself before he sorts out his own mess. She finds this attention endearing. Even more endearing is the cup of coffee they enjoy as if they had just said goodbye to the Willards whose son they had just discussed.

It's only on her drive home that she is able to engage with her epiphany. She hasn't become bored with being a dominatrix. She doesn't need to settle down, and she is certainly not obsessed with North. She has just always afforded herself the experiences she has wanted to have, provided the opportunity presented itself. And Principal North was an opportunity that presented itself. She wanted to know what he might feel like, and now she did. Of course, he felt fucking good and so she definitely would want to be feeling more of him in the future, perhaps with her in charge. The thought of disciplining a school principal excites her.

So there was nothing to panic about. She wasn't having a crisis. She was just processing the new experience that she was preparing to have. And now that she had had it, she could file it appropriately and move on to even greater experiences. Life really was opening itself up to Laura in ways that even she could not have dreamed of. That Jonathan would find his way to their little book club and suddenly be available to her was definitely karma returning some of the favors she'd done in the past. And at this rate, it seemed that karma and Miss Laura would be formidable allies...

6 THE LANDSCAPERS

It is for this reason and nothing else that Dalton, her soon-to-be ex-husband cannot resist one final mounting of the Greek beauty that had married him after just two months and given him the most beautiful children in the land, according to one industry tabloid that profiled the Rothschilds a few years earlier. She had also given him twenty years of her life.

This is the last thing on his mind though as he fumbles with his buckle, his urgency out of place since it was just the two of them in the mansion and from what she knew he had nothing scheduled for the rest of the afternoon despite it being Tuesday. She bends down to help him, biting his cock over the trousers to appease the beast straining against the Armani. A moment later, Dalton's dick hangs above her head, pointing straight out in front of him. She opens her mouth and wets the already wet cock.

Dalton usually enjoys the sheer spectacle of Helena eating his dick, but today, after just a few short jabs in the back of her throat, he pulls her to her feet, fingers her pussy briefly to check for moisture and uses his free hand to guide his cock into his wife. She holds on to his shoulders, losing her balance for the force of his entry. Helena lifts herself off the ground and wraps her toned legs around Dalton, letting his dick go all the way up her cunt.

He carries his wife the short distance to the bed and proceeds to fuck her with the urgency of a man on death row whose last meal was pussy. She catches him staring at his own reflection a few times in the large mirror on the wall behind them but dismisses his distraction for stress. She always put his quirks down to stress. So she just settles herself comfortably under her man and lets him do what he needs to do.

As her cunt moistens, Dalton can go deeper and deeper, the excitement showing in the urgency of his thrusts. He grabs her under her arms, pulling down on her shoulders, forcing her onto his cock, forcing himself completely inside her with every thrust. He goes on like this for several minutes, his thrusts wild and complete. She has completely surrendered herself to him, performing her duty in her classically submissive style.

It's less than thirty minutes to climax. It takes less than ten for him to be hard and inside her again. This time though, he seems to hint at the possibility of lovemaking as compared with the recent fucking. Again, she allows him to lead her where his cock wants to go, and pretty soon, he is panting in a sweaty heap on top of her. She has sort of cum, not enough for her to feel like she's had an orgasm. She guides Dalton's hand to her pussy, a signal he knows to mean she is in need of some assistance getting to the other side.

His index finger finds the inside of her cunt, and she squeezes herself onto it. He pulls it out almost completely and then back inside. He holds her down, one hand on her stomach as he speeds up the exit/entry strategy of his finger, the liquid dripping now from her cunt exciting him. His cock is soon hard again, a deep red from all the pussy munching it's been doing. She spreads her legs and digs her heels into the mattress as the last rigorous stabs from Dalton's finger let her reach her climax. He licks the product of his undertaking from his wife's thighs and cunt as he dips his cock into her mouth.

Helena's tongue embraces the shaft as tenderly as she might have done a snowflake. She's always loved the taste and feel of Dalton's dick. It was solid penis with incredible stamina. It fit perfectly in her mouth and even with its large head lodged in the back of her throat, it was comfortable. She enjoyed the look on his face when she took it into herself entirely, a look that said that he too enjoyed the show. It isn't long before Dalton's third and final load is shot into her mouth, and they both lie briefly together, exhausted. A moment later, they're both showered, and Dalton has grabbed his keys and kissed her goodbye.

Dalton's scent still hangs heavy in the room, the taste of his semen still lingering in the back of Helena's throat despite the repeated rinse and gargle, when the doorbell rings. She walks down the stairs in her see-through sheer throw which she almost let fall to the floor as their family attorney hands her an envelope and asks her to sit down before opening it. It takes several readings and two cups of tea for Helena to realize that she is getting divorced.

The Recovery Position
The divorce is settled quickly. Helena

does it out of shock, and Dalton just wants to avoid a scandal and further interruptions to his new life with his new wife. There is nothing in the settlement that Helena requests that isn't granted. Dalton even throws in some added extras to the tune of a few million. It's clear that he wants no further contact with Helena after this, and so he sets her up for the rest of her life, and beyond, should they ever find an elixir of life that leads to immortality. Suffice it to say, Helena will never need money again.

It doesn't take too long for her to realize that her life constituted largely of the items that were in Dalton's diary. And without Dalton, there really wasn't much for her to do. Her children were away at school most of the time, and so, except for the holidays, she really had little to do for them as well. Her days are suddenly filled with wonderings of what exactly it is that she will do with herself now that she has nobody but herself really to care for. The money does make it easier as her wonderings resemble extravagant shopping sprees rather closely.

Fortunately, having the kids away so long does mean that when they come back it's quite an event. This summer, they'll both be coming home with a set of friends each, and so at least, Helena can busy herself preparing the house for them. The grounds do need some work and the swimming pool has been neglected over the last while, but now that the holidays are close and the summer is officially here, these things can offer up the distraction they need to be now, as opposed to the necessary inconvenience they've been for years.

The bell at the gate sends soft chimes throughout the house, the sound finding Helena in the sunroom where she scribbles notes on a pad as she scans the expansive backyard. The grounds of the property are unnecessarily large, but such was the standard in the O.C. Helena walks though the house to the front foyer to see who is at her gate. She presses a button and the monitor in front of her buzzes to life.

The visuals on the screen reveal a truck. She can't make out the occupants, and they seem unable to work the system because she can't hear a word they're saying. They also don't seem to see the button she keeps telling them to press. Dalton had insisted on the complex system, and now, for the first time, the point Helena had tried to make before installing it, that it would just result in them having to walk to the gate anyway, was now being proven. Pity Dalton wasn't around for a little 'I told you so'.

The sun beats generously down on

Helena as the sexy Greek goddess glides down her limestone driveway towards the gate. The sun reflecting on the stone makes it appear as though she is walking on water. Through her sunglasses, she can see that the truck on the other side of her gate has three men in it. There seem to be tools in the back, but from what she can tell, nothing that could handle the scale of the operation that is the maintenance of her grounds. But she's already close enough to them for them to speak to her without shouting, and so she lets them make their pitch.

The three Latinos are young, in their twenties she thinks, incredibly well built, tan and very handsome. They look like they could have stepped off of the pages of a magazine, or off of the silver screen. They're slightly sunburned though, noticeable despite their tans, and also, they wear vests that make them appear more like construction workers than movie stars, and so the fantasy soon fades. Helena lets them in more for her own amusement than the possibility of actually hiring them, her pad already scribbled with a note for her to call her usual landscapers. But having had such little human company over the last while, the staff on a paid vacation, she takes advantage of the opportunity.

They walk over the grounds, and Helena

watches as each of them seems to focus on a different aspect of the work that needs to be done. They query her on some details that she remembers from her notes, and since she didn't show them the notes, she is impressed by the attention to detail they display. It dawns on her that it might not be a bad idea after all to give them the job. Besides, having these buff young bloods to look at for a few days isn't such a bad thing. It will give her the kind of entertainment she needs right now, without her having to leave her house.

Eduardo seems to be the eldest, or at least the one in charge. He has them unpacking and moving their minimal equipment and starts to give them basic instructions. He is just over thirty, six feet tall with slightly slanting eyes and a wide smile. He has full lips framed by a neatly trimmed mustache and beard. His hands seem ever so slightly too large, his fingers wrapping easily around tools and moving heavy equipment easily. His strength is obvious, even in the authority of his voice.

Luigi resembles the other two but not closely. It isn't just because they are all Latinos, but he looks like he could be their cousin. He is. Pedro and Eduardo are brothers. Luigi is as tall as Eduardo, clean face, wide eyes and a serious mouth with the hint of a smile. But when he laughs, he makes the others burst into laughter for his laughter. He seems to get immense pleasure either from working on gardens and swimming pools, or he just really enjoys the company of his cousins. He is actually the humor in the trio despite his stern demeanor.

The youngest is Pedro, a tower of a man. At twenty-three, he stands a full seven feet. He is lank and skinny with a sheepish face, the innocence of youth. But there is nothing innocent about the young man who appears so soft and likable on the outside. He has already thrown more than just a suggestive glance at Helena, Eduardo reprimanding him several times in the hour or so that they've been there. The truth is all three of them have stolen glances at the beauty.

Helena makes them a tray of drinks and sets it up under the gazebo by the pool house. She then finds a place on an upstairs balcony, ever so slightly out of sight, and watches them work. She allows herself to entertain fantasies that she would never have done while she was married. But now, with the freedom that comes with the absence of a diamond on her left hand, she watches as the vests come off and are pulled through loops on the too-tight jeans the men in her garden below are wearing.

As the fantasy in her head starts to take shape, Helena has her hands on her breasts as she watches the sweat roll down the backs of her gardeners. The sun on their skin turns them into a glowing threesome, ripped and toned, moving as much through the rays as underneath them. The heat of the day is slowly mimicked by Helena's cunt, and she quickly goes to find the toy she given by a 'close friend', a large flesh-colored tool, a modest eight-inch rubber cock. In the current situation, she would need no more.

She is grateful that she has not lost the habit of not wearing underwear at home because the expensive silks she dons her cunt with would just get between her pussy and the vibrator in her hand. She watches Pedro intently, the tallest, as he works on the shrubs closest to her. The other two are uninteresting for the moment as they work on her lawn, disappearing around hedges and rosebushes. Helena has to use her imagination mostly now as the men in her garden are suddenly distracted by the reason they're here. The vibrator is all the way inside her when she zeros in on Pedro, making him the center of her fantasy.

The lanky Latino is almost spiderlike as he moves quickly over the shrubs. Even with her mind and body lost in fantasy and pleasure, the sculpted greenery that emerges from Pedro's scissors confirms for Helena just how unkempt the garden was. The skill Pedro displays with the shears is equal to the skill he displays with his cock as each stroke, each hot sweaty thrust, every long deep penetrating insertion brings her closer and closer to climax. She closes her eyes after taking a final snapshot of the man fucking her in her mind under the sweltering sun.

The vision in her head of Pedro fucking her with all the romance of an exotic lover on a beach in some far off place where palm trees and clear waters are standard truths on every brochure brings her to a perfect climax. Not once does she open her eyes to reaffirm his chest, or his height, the color of his hair or the beads trickling down his back and brow in the early sun. She has enough stored memory for the entire experience. With her eyes closed, she is unaware that Pedro has himself caught a glimpse of her through the moldings of the stone balustrade, her hand's position and movements giving away her deed. But for the duration of the workday, he makes no mention of this, and so Helena is blissfully unaware that she was spotted.

When she suggested that they use the bathroom in the pool house to wash up before lunch, the last thing she expected was that they would use the shower for its original purpose, and so when she enters to find three totally naked men in the pool house, she almost drops the tray. They stand in the living area, in all their glory, cooling themselves in the generous breeze that fills the living area from the direction of the ocean. Eduardo apologizes for the wet floor before he apologizes for being naked. The others suddenly realize their own nakedness and half-reach for towels, half grabbing them, half covering their cocks. Helena puts the tray down and forces her gaze on the horizon, trying not to stare.

Pedro has of course informed the others of what he saw, and so now that she is in front of them, their cocks hanging before her, they reach for their generous meat and hold on to the dicks in a mock attempt to hide them, the towels suddenly needing to hang over their shoulders. Helena is experienced enough to know that this is pure showoff. She has no problem with the display and so lets her eyes do what the dicks in front of them expect. Suddenly, more of each cock reaches through the fingers wrapped around them.

Helena smiles as they look at her with eyes she's seen a million times. Men have always wanted to fuck her. They can't help it. This reaction she's gotten from men her whole life makes her wonder why it is that she now stands in her pool house, divorced and wanting to be fucked sideways by men who've come to tend to her gardens and put the sparkle back into her swimming pool. Her divorce hadn't really affected her as she had expected it to, especially with all the horror stories that she had been told by friends who themselves were still happily married. In fact, the one feeling that she hadn't allowed herself to feel, to acknowledge even, was the feeling that now stirred in her in the presence of unfamiliar cock: Freedom!

Since she met Dalton, she had not seen or touched another penis, except her son's, but that really didn't count in the current circumstance. When Eduardo offers their services beyond just her lawn and pool, a whole new world suddenly opens up in Helena's head. Suddenly, a simple yes could mean that she would be fucked to her heart's content by three virile young men who found her attractive enough to make the offer, attractive enough to have their cocks standing solid at the mention of fucking her. This world had never occurred to her save for during naughty chats on girl's night. But now, this world had made a very sudden appearance in her pool house. The two worlds had merged.

Briefly, the thought that she couldn't

possibly do anything of this nature surfaces, but then the realization that she brought herself to a climax earlier with imaginings of a penis that looks quite close to the real thing kicks that thought to the curb. Three uncircumcised dicks, long, thick and hard, circle her and she knows that what happens next is up to her. She has given no indication to proceed but has also done nothing to let them know that the removal of her light covering is unacceptable. There are four naked bodies in the breeze as the pool house protects them from the heat outside. The heat inside, on the other hand, is intensifying.

Eduardo's fingers dig into Helena's shoulders, and the surrender is immediate. She had never anticipated just how much she needed to be touched until she was. He massages her with an intentional technique, a rhythm that is both rehearsed and perfectly paced. Eduardo is not touching her out of gratitude or because she might pay them more if he does it well. He is touching her because there is nothing else he wants to do right now. This was how Dalton touched her, even on that last afternoon. He had wanted to. Eduardo now wants to.

Luigi sucks on her breasts, and then takes them into his hands. There are no question marks in her mind as Luigi's lips, soft and thick, answer all her breast's requests. There is a similar intentionality in his hands to the one exhibited by Eduardo, and Helena knows that these men have pleased many women. It is her that is grateful for the sheer possibility of them, a possibility that the lack of resistance is turning into a very present reality.

The only fumbling fingers are Pedro's. Their not inexperienced, just excited. He's clearly taken by surprise that the scenario that he had dared present to the others is actually happening. His fingers are on her cunt and then in it: all in, and then all out. Pedro fingers her cunt as if his task is to take her temperature. The long fingers go all the way inside her where they wait for a reading. The extraction is slow and complete. He waits briefly and then reinserts his thermometers, each one confirming the reading of the previous one.

Pedro allows for Luigi to take licks of her cunt when he removes his finger. Sometimes, Luigi's tongue stays on the external surface of the cunt while Pedro's fingers work the inside. Eduardo seems content with the totality of her body as he massages every available inch of her. Helena has no idea of who is where, her eyes closed and her focus on the sensation with little care for who is actually doing what. It seems okay for her to keep this entire experience about her, even with the occasional cock prodding her but making no threatening gestures.

Pedro's fingers make the migration to her ass as Luigi monopolizes her pussy. The hot tongue also seems to have no designs on the inside of the cunt as the outside of it provides sufficient entertainment. The fingers in her ass go on a double date as Pedro sends two in at a time. Helena doesn't resist, her focus on the mouth on her pussy. She is so close to orgasm now that even as Pedro moves his fingers around in her ass and Luigi licks her cunt like a schoolboy with a popsicle in summer, she feels nothing but the sensation and loses the awareness of the tools creating it.

Eduardo has taken it upon himself to keep her up. His arms are under Helena's, and his hands are on her breasts. There is no space for cock on the essential parts of Helena, and so she anticipates none. But those parts are being dealt with so expertly that they are not complaining, and so neither is Helena. The tri-cock alliance also seems in no hurry for any real invasion, and so they give all their attention to providing an expertly engineered orgasm to the woman already panting under their touch.

Helena is aware of her orgasm more

than she is of who it is that is giving it to her. All she knows is that for the first time since her divorce she is having a fucking fantastic orgasm and that nothing about the experience is about anyone but her. She couldn't be bothered, as she climaxes, what the three men who had come to tend to her gardens think of her when they leave, or even if they come back the next day. For now, as she lays alone on the chaise taking in the lingering scent of the exotic cocks that just explored every possibility of her pussy, she is convinced once more that she is still very much a woman.

Breaststroke

Whatever doubts she had about them returning are put to rest when Helena opens the gate for her gardeners just before seven. There is nothing awkward about the way they greet her, and there are also no snide remarks, sneers or snickers as they meet her in the foyer. Pedro, Luigi and Eduardo stand in front of her like three men here to do a job, and whatever yesterday was seems to have remained there, in yesterday. She silently appreciates this.

Helena offers them breakfast on the lower terrace that overlooks the gardens. Already, the property looks immaculate, the details visible only to those whose job it is to fix them. Clearly, the three are perfectionists. They discuss these details over the fruit, croissants and coffee that make up the end of breakfast after the bacon and eggs. Helena is as impressed with the work they did on her as she is with what they are doing on her property. But the work on her cunt isn't up for discussion, something that seems to have unanimous approval. She clears up as the men get to work.

She is unable to watch them work today so she busies herself with the admin of the inside of her home. Staff needs to be recalled, and so she starts to make the necessary phone calls. She also has to decide on how she will keep herself busy while her children are entertaining their friends, not wanting to be the annoying mother who was always hanging around. Occasionally, she catches her gardeners through the window as they focus on tasks she can't even figure out. All she knows really is that whatever they're doing, the results are absolutely beautiful.

Three in the afternoon comes sooner than even Luigi, Pedro and Eduardo thought it should, and so they linger briefly in the shower before getting dressed and making their way to the van. They pack up the equipment that they will be taking with them, some tools needing oiling and maintenance which they will do at home overnight. They jump into the van and head for the gate, moving slowly as they anticipate the closed gate to give way.

Helena stands behind the truck, just out of view, the remote in hand. She is still not sure what a conversation would comprise of now because the thoughts in her head she dares not voice, nobody having made any indication of a desire for a continuation, or at the very least a replay of the foreplay. There can be no more present tension than the tension between her thighs, and all she wants to do is stop them from leaving. It's not desperation; just desire, the desire to explore her freedom further.

She eventually wills herself to open the gate, and Eduardo checks in the rearview to see whether she's used the remote or done the opening from inside. He catches her in the mirror, pointing the remote at the truck unnecessarily. Luigi and Pedro see what Eduardo is looking at, and they get him to stop the vehicle. No question comes to mind immediately, but Eduardo opens the door and jumps out, Helena already walking to him.

'Will that be all ma'am?' he manages at last.

'It doesn't have to be', Helena can't help it.

She presses the remote and watches the gate close. Helena is unsure what she's

just done, or even what she is about to do.
What she knows is that even if she does
nothing, what the three men who are all
suddenly walking towards her will do to
her will be all the doing she needs. She
turns and walks up the few steps to the
front door and then into the house. She
doesn't look back as she walks up the
stairs.

Helena has had the lust inside her
brewing since she had her cunt and ass
assaulted by the three men who are on
their way up to her bedroom. She removes
the little she has on and gets onto the bed,
remembering briefly the last time she was
naked on it, and suddenly needing to
make it so that Dalton isn't the last man
that fucked her on it. She knows from the
look on the faces of the men who start to
undress as soon as they see her that this
is exactly what is about to happen.

On the bed, the three fight for her
mouth. Their tongues are on her neck,
then on the side of her face, before finding
her lips and then the inside of her mouth.
If they could all kiss her at the same time
then this is what they would do. They
come very close to doing just that, but
soon settle for the fact that while they
can't all kiss her beautiful mouth at the
same time, they can all kiss her at once
provided they kissed her in different
places. Pedro, Luigi and Eduardo are all

expert kissers.

Eduardo wins out over Helena's mouth. As he lets her take his tongue into it, her breasts welcome his hands. She is on his chest, her head tilted back so that if her eyes were open she would be looking into his. His soft mouth on hers makes her eyes impossible to open. Eduardo rests one arm under her so that his hand plays gently with her hip, the other hand playing up and down her belly and over her beautiful breasts. Luigi and Pedro have parted her legs enough so that they are able to comfortably kiss her from her feet, up her leg past her knees, onto her thighs, then her inner thigh whereupon they meet at her rapidly moistening vagina. They do the gentlemanly thing and let whoever arrives at her pussy first take the first lick.

The hands and lips moving over her body soon converge on her pussy and become tongues. Helena's cunt is triple licked with such precision that the absence of sensation on the other parts of her isn't noticed. Her entire body becomes a highly charged sexual organ as each lick sends tremors through her that would register on the Richter scale. Her legs are parted wider now, having to accommodate the length of both Luigi and Pedro's shoulders. Eduardo has given himself a better vantage, hanging his cock over her head and coming at her pussy from up top. He is rewarded with Helena's mouth around his hard, heavy meat.

A finger finds her ass. It isn't a violating finger, but more like a gentle explorer. At no point does Helena feel like a bitch being fucked. Every single touch, every kiss and every insertion, every single lick and every suggestion of things to come are all indicative of absolute appreciation for what she is letting them have. Eduardo, Luigi and even the over-enthusiastic Pedro are in awe of the magnificent gift that is the almost ethereal body of the now ex Mrs. Rothschild. More fingers find the tight hole at the centre of her firm, toned ass. But again, they are not scrambling, fumbling fingers forcing entry. Each one of the appendages waits its turn and then makes a careful, gentle, delicious exploration of the tight space.

There is a slightly less gentlemanly demeanor when these same thirty soldiers discover her pussy. The tender pink flesh is immediately pulled apart so that the path into it is perfectly clear. One by one, the fingers make inroads and bring her wet pussy to a tantalizing tingle. Helena can still not bring herself to open her eyes, she can't bring herself to open her inner world to the reality of the outer, wanting instead to make this a game she played alone. She lets her mind decide whose finger has entered and stirred, lingered and then allowed itself to be joined by another. She lets her pussy decide which one of the men on her bed has dared pull her vagina apart so firmly that even in the absence of cock she suddenly feels occupied.

There is no denying the cock that decides finally to make the first entry. The enthusiastic Pedro feeds Helena a generous serving of his cock, a cunt-full she gladly swallows. Pedro's smooth dick makes a total advancement into the tempered vagina and then he thrusts his head into her rear walls. Not once does he pull his cock out more than an inch, his signature style more of a battering as opposed to a stroking. He pounds the back of Helena's cunt with his large head, the shaft doing little more than line the inside of her vagina.

Eduardo takes the next cock shift. Pedro's withdrawal is seamless though, and Helena has no idea initially that the cock inside her is a different cock. But when the cock doesn't reach the back of her cunt, but instead pushes the entire length of her passage outward, she knows this is someone else. She correctly guesses that it is Eduardo despite the fact that her eyes are still not open. Eduardo is heavier than the others, and he lets his entire weight drive his thick cock into Helena. Unlike Pedro, Eduardo uses the full mobility of his midsection to send his cock all the way in and all the way out of Helena, instantly providing a more dynamic fuck.

Despite his aggressive strokes, Eduardo's cock is relentless. And so is his energy. He drives his dick into Helena with an unceasing enthusiasm, an unwavering determination to bring the most out of her cunt. He succeeds, repeatedly, bringing her to three orgasms before he eventually pulls out, knowing that he is still too far from climax but that Luigi is losing patience, his own cock needing a dance in the warm depths of Helena's matured cunt.

The only difference between Luigi's cock and Pedro's is length. The two dicks are exactly the same shape, the same girth, but Pedro's has a full three inches on Luigi's. Even their style of fucking is similar, Luigi reaching the back of Helena easily even with the deficit. But to the back-wall pounding, Luigi adds an upward stroke at the end of each pound. His solid dick head pushes into the soft rear of the vagina and then runs up the wall before retreating. Each upward stroke draws a moan from Helena and Luigi knows he's hit her spot. He continues to hit it until he leads her to her umpteenth orgasm and his first. He is the first to cum, and the first to make for the bathroom to deal with the relevant admin.

Pedro takes immediate advantage of the available cunt, Helena giving no indication that she needs a break. Inside her, he goes for the back, trying for the moans that Luigi managed to get so effortlessly. When none but the standard husky breathing is forthcoming, Pedro's ego has him thrust harder into the almost fragile Helena, a move that has her wrap her legs around his and squeeze hard enough for him to halt his attack. He apologizes with a long passionate kiss, the deep kind that relaxes her legs enough for his cock to once again make a solid invasion. But with his lips on hers, their tongues locked, his egotistical stabbings are suddenly acceptable.

Pedro eventually shoots, accepting that he is not Luigi. He makes room for Eduardo, the only one still to shoot, and goes to take care of the condom now half hanging off his limp cock. Luigi stands near the foot of the bed pulling on his own meat, hard and uncovered. Eduardo has Helena alone on the bed now, and if his previous attempt at her vagina was anything to go by, he'd need to have her to himself, at least for a while. He widens her cunt slowly, driving his thick cock into her as though her salivating pussy was bone dry. As slowly, he pulls his fat rod out of her. Slowly, he inserts the cock again, and slowly, he withdraws it. With every withdrawal, he uses a towel thrown to him by Pedro, also now watching the scene from the base of the bed, to wipe Helena's excess lust from his cock. He uses his dick to rid the cunt of just enough of the juice to make his navigation of the void effective.

Driving his dick into the now significantly drier cunt, Eduardo reaches down and takes Helena's mouth into his. His cock is grateful for the new work environment and shows this by swelling to half an additional inch in girth, and stretching an unexpected four additional inches in length. Helena pulls her mouth from Eduardo's so that she can let out the necessary gasp. He allows her a moment and for a minute does nothing, but then resumes his thrusts, slowly. He has lost his earlier aggression and makes a sensual infiltration of the inner workings of a now hot-as-hell Helena. She takes his legs in hers, wrapping herself around him. But unlike with Pedro, her intention is to draw him into her, completely. Eduardo's dick obliges her, completely.

The moans from Helena let everyone in the room know that Eduardo and Luigi both now know her pussy's secret. Pedro and Luigi each take a leg in hand and move them off Eduardo and away from him. Helena bends her knees, exposing her maximum depths to the cock inside her that quickly takes full advantage of this. Eduardo's complete weight is not uncomfortable on the woman, the deal between them having been made by cock and cunt. The kisses on her ankles and then up to her thighs are just what Eduardo needs because as Luigi and Pedro shoot gentle shots of pleasure across her entire nervous system Helena's cunt does a series of involuntary squeeze/releases on his supersized cock. It takes a few minutes at most, but Eduardo is soon sending his dick into Helena with the aggression he had the first time, and this time, she absolutely loves it.

Pedro makes for her mouth, and she turns to the side so that she can take his cock into her mouth. Eduardo allows for the strain of her neck by turning himself onto his side and taking her leg over his. He takes a firm hold of her thigh and sends his cock into her while at the same time lifting himself off her other leg ever so slightly. His maximum weight would cut off her circulation in minutes, and this is the last thing they need. Pedro is grateful for Eduardo's adjustment since he can now fuck Helena's mouth without having to contort himself into a pretzel. Luigi takes the opportunity that is now availed by the new access to her ass.

There is no part of Helena that isn't

drenched in sweat. Everyone around her is dripping in sweat. The deodorant from each of the men has merged and fused and become something interesting with the perfume and oils on Helena, and this scent, along with the heavy smell of super fucking, hangs in the air. Luigi doesn't have any difficulty entering Helena, laying himself behind her and filling her asshole with his cock as Eduardo's thick meat gives her vagina a second's relief. He waits for a further second so that Luigi can withdraw before sending his cock into her again, both Luigi and Eduardo's cocks trying to find each other inside Helena.

All three cocks enter their respective holes at the same time, in military unison. If they were all to levitate suddenly, they would perfectly suspend Helena on three solid dicks. Despite their individual cum thresholds, they've all three decided to bring Helena to a final orgasm first, and so they all keep the pace steady and progressive for nobody's sake but Helena's. There are doubts even in Helena's head that she will be able to reach another orgasm, but the three keep at it anyway, fucking mouth, ass and cunt with thick, long Latino cocks that have stood firm in the Los Angeles heat.

Pedro is the first to shoot, Helena's hot mouth too much for him. Helena swallows his load before he even registers his orgasm, and so he continues to thrust into her mouth for a while still after his load has disappeared down her throat. Pedro lets out a grunt, and Luigi makes for his own finish. He cannot keep Eduardo's pace and thrusts into Helena's ass with a new vigor. She knows that her climax is reliant on the cock in her pussy pounding at a perfect and steady pace, and so she lets her focus fall on Eduardo while Luigi does what he has to. Luigi shoots his hot load into her after a couple of deep thrusts.

Luigi and Pedro let their cocks hang where they land. Both dicks remain hard in the warm places they occupy while Eduardo starts to work himself up, knowing that Helena is now his sole responsibility. Helena is also aware that Eduardo's cock is her responsibility, and since he has yet to cum, she suddenly feels the pressure. She decides not to try anything fancy and to focus instead on keeping her cunt as receptive as possible so that Eduardo can send his cock into the places inside her that will help him along. Her own orgasm comes before his though and she lets out a loud scream, almost biting onto Pedro's cock and squeezing the last jizz from Luigi's as her entire body goes into an orgasmic spasm.

Eduardo pushes so hard into Helena as he finally starts to sense his impending climax that she falls back onto Luigi who falls almost flat on his back. Pedro follows Helena's mouth, his cock already ready for a little mini climax due to the constant contact with Helena's tongue. If it wasn't for Helena, Eduardo would quite completely be fucking the living shit out of Luigi, who has no choice but to take the weight of both Helena, which is negligible, and Eduardo, not so negligible. But the complete penetration his cock has now achieved has him too bracing for a mini climax, thanks to the tightness and heat of Helena's ass, and the powerful thrusting of Eduardo, which is moving Helena perfectly over his cock.

Helena, Pedro and Luigi all have mini orgasms before Eduardo finally reaches his apex, sending his cock almost through Helena and splitting the walls of her pussy so that her cunt rains love over his cock which has soaked itself in cum. Eduardo's cock runs the length of Helena's vagina for another half hour before he has satisfied himself that the insides of his Latino torpedo are dried out. As a courtesy, all three continue gentle thrusts until they are sure that Helena is absolutely satisfied. They withdraw their cocks, all still hard but themselves satisfied, and watch as Helena curls up into a ball and tries to find herself in her head, her eyes closed and her hand on her pussy, which beats loudly and sends her into little jerks every time she touches her clit. It will be a while before she is completely gathered and so the men do what they must and leave.

Marco Polo

Helena walks out onto the terrace and looks out over the perfectly manicured grounds. The place looks immaculate. It is immaculate. It's been barely a couple of weeks, and the entire property has never looked better. The swimming pool looks summer ready and were it not for the bell Helena might have thrown herself into the water already, despite it being just a little after six. It's a little early for the gardening threesome, but since this is their last day, they've decided to get an early start so that they've finished the bulk of the work by the time the sun is at its harshest. They're gunning for noon.

Helena herself has never felt better, and this has nothing to do with the fact that the kids will arrive in two days. The property is ready to receive them. The house too will be ready, the entire place scheduled for a complete once over tomorrow, when the in-house staff arrives. Helena opens the gate from inside and then leaves the front door ajar. Luigi, Pedro and Eduardo are familiar with the house now, and so there is no longer any need for formalities, on the last day least of all. The three find her on the terrace and join in her admiration of their work, particularly the swimming pool.

The four of them have really enjoyed each other. It's been a new and exhilarating experience for Helena. She's learned new things about herself and her body, and she has had her attractiveness confirmed, although she has never doubted it, not even after getting divorced. Eduardo, Luigi and Pedro have had fun confirming Helena's womanhood for her, something they've probably done a few times for a few other women, but will never mention to Helena, knowing that most women are sensitive about such things. But Helena Maropis isn't most women. And in her single state, she has no intention of ever being most women again.

She hits the water after she has served her gardeners their last breakfast in her house. They eat while discussing the little bit that remains to be done, and so since this has nothing to do with her and requires zero input from her, the water is where she most wants to be. It proves to be everything its appearance promises, and Helena stays under the surface of the water for as long as possible, wishing that she was able to breathe underwater, the cool liquid on her skin warm and comforting. She gazes at the morning sun high above her and eventually raises her head to meet its rays, which dance on the surface of the pool and warm it slightly.

She's been in the water for about an hour when she suddenly realizes that she has an audience. The three stand on the terrace, watching her in the water. The sun has not yet made clear its intention, and the three on the terrace are covered in the shadow of the house such that Helena has to squint to see who stands where, Pedro the only obvious one for his height. They want to join her, but this would defeat the purpose of arriving so early. She's enjoying her new 'fuck it' attitude and disappears beneath the surface, reemerging with her bikini in her hand. Only Eduardo uses the stairs to get to the pool, Luigi and Pedro scaling the balustrade.

Everyone in the pool is naked. This was easily achieved since the men had nothing but shorts and vests on. Today was really just about removing the bags of rubble that contained the waste from the expert work they had done. These items of clothing were now on the grass just beyond the limestone, too close to the water not to get wet. They immediately go for Helena, circling her, their eyes scanning the area for onlookers, feeling very exposed suddenly. Helena reassures them, explaining the design of the house and how only people on the property had a view of the pool, and since they are the only people on the property, nobody can see them.

Eduardo takes up his favorite position, behind her, his cock against her ass, between her cheeks, stiffening quickly. His cock is too thick to even consider entering her tight ass, water not being the best lubricant for this exercise. Even with a good lubricant, his meat would probably be a bit too much for the demure little asshole. So Eduardo just enjoys running his shaft between Helena's cheeks, holding her buns and pushing them together against his cock. His thrusting makes Helena want him in her cunt almost immediately.

Pedro beats him to it though, already entering Helena from the front. His long shaft finds her cunt easily and makes its entry as Pedro moves closer to her. By the time her breasts are touching his chest, his cock is almost completely inside her, Eduardo almost losing his position as Helena is lifted slightly higher that his cock is comfortable with. They make a short move to shallower water and everyone is happy again. Pedro immediately starts fucking Helena, a vision in the blue with the sun dancing through her hair.

Eduardo makes his way to the steps that lead out of the pool, followed by Luigi who knows that Eduardo was always the best choreographer of such scenes that might otherwise be awkward. Pedro now has Helena around his waist, fucking her as he wades towards the other two, Eduardo sitting on the steps, Luigi standing in front of him. Pedro gets between them and gives Eduardo his back. He lifts Helena off his cock and then parts his long legs so that Eduardo is between them. Helena eases herself gently onto Eduardo's thick meat, taking it into her pussy easier than any of them had anticipated. Eduardo gives a few of his signature thrusts, wetting the inside of Helena's cunt quickly.

Pedro holds his long cock and points it down towards Helena's pussy. Pedro's shaft then hitches a ride on Eduardo's, and after finding his balance, Pedro's dick is resting on top of Eduardo's and both cocks are splitting Helena's perfect pussy so that her moans are ecstatic screams. She looks down at the double-dick invasion, and her cunt spills generous volumes of lubricant so that the cocks soon have complete reign of her vagina. Helena takes control of the movement when she realizes that both men are taking strain in their attempt to keep her filled with cock. He plays her role so well that neither Eduardo nor Pedro even needs to move as Helena fucks the shit out their solid cocks.

Luigi gives her just enough time to get comfortable with her double-horsy ride before he finally sends his own cock into her ass. Helena's riding gives him some friction but because her focus is underneath herself and in front of herself, Luigi has to thrust into her in order to satisfy his cock. He can go surprisingly deep into her tight hole with all her attention being on her cunt. Helena never once lets Luigi know that anything about his massive cock so deep up inside her ass is unwelcomed. She has never been so fully fucked up the rear but neither has her pussy been so incredibly infiltrated. Again, the threesome has given her a first experience, and again it is blowing her mind.

Helena has her first orgasm, the double rod inside her finding her g-spot and not leaving it until she merges her pussy fluids with the water in the pool. Everyone knows the capability of Eduardo's cock, so it is Pedro who withdraws, moving up one-step and to the side of Eduardo so that he can feed Helena his cock without hanging his ass and nuts over his brother's face. Helena holds onto Pedro at the waist as he feeds half his shaft to her. Luigi continues fucking her ass, providing just enough movement for Eduardo's cock to be happy, Eduardo not needing to move himself to create the pleasure on his meat that comes from its interaction with the inside of Helena.

Luigi takes Helena's head into his hands and pulls it back so that Pedro's cock is left wanting. He kisses her on her lips while driving his cock into her harder, faster. Deeper and deeper, faster and faster, Luigi thrusts until he can hold out no longer. He sends his cock, and his load into Helena while sucking hard on her tongue. He then releases her mouth and kisses the side of her neck and then her back, his cock remaining where it is for the moment. His hands find her breasts, and he gives the mounds the gentlest strokes while he trusts his now flaccid penis in her, but not out.

Helena's mouth works on Pedro's cock almost as soon as it is free from Luigi's lips. Pedro does little moving, simply planting his penis as deep into Helena's mouth as she will allow, and then leaving the rest up to her. Helena lets her tongue run up and down the meat in her mouth, and sucks on it as though she were drinking through a rather large straw. Pedro immediately shoots some jizz onto her tongue. She sucks harder, pulls the cock deeper, and runs her tongue around it a little faster. Pedro gives up more of his load. He holds onto her head when he can no longer hold out and fucks her mouth rapidly until the total sum of his cum is shot into her mouth and swallowed.

Eduardo stands up slowly, and Luigi takes his place on the steps. Neither Luigi's nor Eduardo's cocks leaves the hole it is in. Pedro lies down next to Luigi and takes Helena's lips between his teeth before letting his tongue find hers. He kisses her with the passion of a familiar lover and the excitement and enthusiasm of a new one. Pedro is the kind of lover who could satisfy you all by himself, and for a moment, Helena entertains this thought. The moment is brief though as Luigi's cock has started to harden in her ass, and Eduardo, who is driving his thick dick into her already, is pushing her ass down on Luigi. The dick in her ass that was so comfortable moments earlier has morphed back into the mammoth Latino mamba that has her ass jam-packed.

Fortunately, Luigi is caught between the steps and Helena and so can do little because of Eduardo driving into her from the top. So Luigi's meat is a stationary soldier positioned more for effect than for effectiveness. Pedro is content with her mouth and his lanky fingers spider over her breasts and belly. Eduardo has his hands planted on the steps to the sides of Luigi's waist, and he sends his tool in long strokes in and out of Helena. The sun beats down on his back and the heat on his skin shoots through his body and finds the heat on his cock. Helena's cunt-juice is super-charged and heated itself so that Eduardo has to remove his cock completely a few times to avoid losing his erection due to overheating.

Pedro's fingers find Helena's clit as Eduardo's thrusts gain momentum. Helena and Luigi both moan now as Eduardo forces his cock into Helena and his self onto both Helena and Luigi. He drives right into her and pushes onto every part of her cunt with every part of his cock so that she loses her sense of where her orgasm is coming from. Deep inside her a river starts to flow and this flow is quickly evolving into an eruption, then a gushing raging torrent as Eduardo sends solid lengths of cock deep into her, breaking down whatever dam walls exist that keep her juices at bay between fucks. Her clit dances under Pedro's fingers, sending the final signals for her dam sluices to open completely.

Luigi takes her hands in his, her mouth still in Pedro's. Her clit and Pedro's fingers become inseparable as Eduardo takes her cunt to a place only a cock as thick as his can. The pressure on her cunt, an outward push coupled with a deep insertion and swift extraction, is an experience given to a pussy only by the thickest dicks. Anyone of the view that size doesn't matter has never been in the presence of a decent sized cock. Because any pussy will tell you, thick dick is good dick. Thick dick understands that there are more places hiding between the folds of a vagina than can be accessed by the longest cocks, so only thick dick provides the pressure on these places from within that completes any orgasm. Skill is largely negligible if one has a cock Like Eduardo. Eduardo is possessed of both size and skill however.

Luigi finds a gap and starts to take stabs into Helena. Eduardo's forward thrusting lifts Helena slightly off his cock and as this happens Luigi thrusts upwards into her. Eduardo and Luigi have found without even trying, the perfect technique for both of their dicks to reach deep into Helena and make a steady beeline for climax. Helena's vagina has already seen the light, and her walls start to come down again, her orgasm taking on its own life as the orgasms of the cocks inside her find their own breaths. Pedro moves up a few steps and again sends his own dick into Helena's mouth, this time though he starts fucking her mouth immediately, his dick getting hard quickly, and his orgasm quickly appearing on the horizon.

All three men are sending their meat into her again, each one focusing more on their own climax now, Helena's in full swing. Luigi is the first to shoot, warming the inside of Helena's ass with his load. Pedro sends a warm river of his juice into her mouth, not as substantial as the first but sufficient to quench her thirst. Eduardo is the final warrior in the battle, not surprisingly. He pushes his arms under hers and lets his hands rest on Luigi's shoulders, needing a solid support now for his advance to the finish line. If he pushed down on the pampered Helena's shoulders as hard as he was now doing on his cousin's, the bruising on her would have been obvious, and suspect. Luigi is a trooper and offers the support his cousin needs.

Pedro removes his cock from Helena's mouth, knowing that now she will need to breathe. He fondles her breasts, Luigi's fingers this time finding her clit. Eduardo stabs into Helena now with more force than any of them have done until now, combined. He drives more dick into her than she's felt even from Pedro. Of course, it is the force of the fucking that creates this illusion, but even so, her cunt believes the lie. Eduardo rams his thick baton right to the back of her cunt until she screams an ecstatic fuck me! Eduardo does just that. He sends his super warrior into her with such force her pussy quakes under him.

Luigi and Pedro are just props now, Eduardo's fucking seemingly endless. Everyone has reached their cum threshold, and so they all just wait for Eduardo, who's cock seems insistent on showing off. His expert dick starts to pull Helena's pussy out of its lull, and soon her cunt is again an active participant in the game played by Eduardo's cock. The other two look on in amazement. They've seen this before, and it gets them every time. Eduardo's stamina and control are superb. The woman he marries one day will have met the fuck match of every female fantasy. Helena audibly surrenders her g-spot to Eduardo, whose cock has brought it out of hiding.

Luigi fucks Helena's ass gently as her moans harden his cock again. Pedro is content just to watch, knowing that she is too close to cumming for him to disrupt her flow. He also doesn't want to do anything that might distract Eduardo, who seems to have settled into a comfortable dash for the end. He sends his shaft into Helena just as she starts her orgasm, her cunt squeezing around his dick so tight that for a second extracting it is impossible. But as her climax continues and her cunt rains over him, he is soon thrusting his way to his own eruption.

He settles his cock in the back of her cunt as his orgasm finally begins. Eduardo knows his cock, and so rests inside her for a minute while his dick builds the necessary impetus. Then without warning, he withdraws completely and kneels on the steps astride Helena, taking his cock in his hand and stroking his dick until he shoots a massive load onto Helena's belly and all around her. He shoots for a full minute before he starts to ease up, and his load dwindles, whereupon she comes up and gives the mammoth cock the gentlest licks, until no more cum drips from it. It's a while before they get out of the water and carry a visibly exhausted but rejuvenated Helena to the pool house.

Freestyle

They stand briefly under the cold water of the shower, then briefly under warmer water. Helena is given generous doses of moisturizer, rubbed into her by many hands. The thirty fingers massaging her find every part of her body that can be charged sexually and they do just that. Soon, her entire body has forgotten every orgasm she's ever had and anticipates what her vagina now believes will be her first. Her cunt is practically drowning in itself from the inside.

Eduardo sends two fingers into her

cunt, her legs parting immediately. She watches his eyes as he watches his fingers. Pedro and Luigi find their cocks in her hands, Helena gently stroking the rock-solid cocks and pulling them so that their owners soon stand and walk to her head, each man at her shoulders. She pulls on the dicks that point towards the ceiling above her eyes. She raises her mouth so that her tongue can reach the large balls hanging ripe above her. Her gaze falls away from Eduardo, who seems to know what he is doing, and she closes her eyes as she sucks gently on the cocooned nuts.

Helena pulls down gently on the cocks so that they follow her as she rests her head back on the pillow on the chaise. Her mouth opens and receives both dicks, Luigi and Pedro helping her by bending their knees slightly and dipping their dicks into her willing mouth. She mouths both cocks simultaneously, the men thrusting down as she sucks them deeper into her. They fit quite comfortably, both their dicks combining to become the girth of Eduardo's, almost. Eduardo really is possessed of the thickest cock Helena has ever dared allow herself to imagine, and with his fingers in her cunt, she finds herself getting wetter at the sheer thought of his uber shaft. His fingers do a significantly stellar job on her vagina though. Her cunt is moist, pulsating each time Eduardo enters, and beating as he exits. His fingers relay this to his cock, which now wants the same attention. But Eduardo has a different idea.

The sight of Helena with the two cocks stuffing her mouth excites him, and Eduardo raises her leg and half turns her over so that her ass is in direct alignment with his cock. He removes his fingers from her cunt, but only so that he can reinsert them from below, still between her legs but just from the back as opposed to the top front entry he had been making. He uses the warm wetness from Helena's pussy to lightly lubricate his cock, which he then positions directly on Helena's asshole. The hole looks like it has never been opened before, a perfect little rosebud. Eduardo pushes his thick man-meat against the hole, which immediately resists, despite it having very recently been dicked.

He lets his fingers work on her cunt a little more, thrusting against her tight hole as he lets his fingers pull her pussy apart. Her vagina is giving, three fingers comfortably dancing around inside it, but her asshole will not budge. It had made room for Luigi, but Eduardo knows that having had visual as well as vaginal confirmation of the massive proportions of his cock, Helena's brain is telling her ass not to let the monster in. But the sight of the dicks in her mouth, the moans of enjoyment from Helena, Luigi and Pedro alike, Eduardo also wants his cock in a hard to reach place. He also wants his dick in a chokehold.

He pulls more liquid from Helena's pussy and this time coats her asshole. He lets his fingers slide in, one from each hand, and then uses these fingers to gently pry the hole apart. As the tiny entrance starts to give, he thrusts towards the darkness, the thick head on his dick lodging tightly in the tiny circle. The fingers make a slow exit as the head of his dick finally disappears into Helena, her moans changed for the new intruder. Eduardo quickly finds her cunt and sends two fingers into it so as to distract her from the full measure of his cock that he is about to send into her ass.

As he rips Helena apart from the back, his fingers do the same in the front. Helena pulls the cocks in her mouth deep down into her throat, not able to comprehend enough to know what to do with her body from the waist down. She had never had this much cock in her rear end, and even for a Greek, this was too much Greek! Eduardo watches the cocks disappearing into her mouth, listens to the excitement from the men. He watches his own cock for a second and then returns his gaze to Helena's mouth, imagining that his own cock has joined the oral brigade. He loses himself in fucking Helena's asshole, his thoughts on her hot mouth, ramming into her ass as though it were suddenly possessed of a tongue and sufficient saliva to make the ramming he was doing possible. Helena doesn't resist, her focus on the double cock fuck happening in her mouth, and the sudden presence of four of Eduardo's fingers in her cunt, his thumb dancing over her clit each time the fingers dig fully into her.

Eduardo doesn't expect it, but suddenly, his cock is filling the inside of Helena's ass with hot liquid. The cream comes out with his cock as he withdraws and then shoots deeper into her. The tight squeeze is what he needed to get to a quick finish. Not that he's in any way finished, mind you, just that he needed to comfort his dick for the visions offered by the other two dicks in the room. They just seemed to be getting the better deal. But Helena's cunt has been satisfied most by one cock: Eduardo's. And now, her ass has proven up to the challenge of bringing him to a swift climax once he has handled her vagina. But having seen what her ass can do, Pedro is quick to want in on the action.

Every dick in the room suits up, making it clear to Helena that this fuck session is about to escalate. Everyone knows even though it hasn't been said, that this is the last time they will probably see each other. They had done a superb job on the gardens, and were it not for the fucking, Helena might have taken them on permanently. But a line has been crossed, and now they just needed to make the best of it. Pedro's long cock pushes easily into Helena. Her ass gives way quickly, but remains tight. She knows this cock and so she accepts it quickly. Pedro thanks her with a series of deep circular thrusts that make her feel like his cock might make an appearance out of her cunt, which Eduardo is now teasing with the head of his cock.

Luigi fucks her mouth steadily, enjoying every corner, every crevice of the hot space. Pedro gives the cue to advance and as the thickness that is Eduardo's fills Helena's vagina, Pedro fills her ass with almost eight inches of his dick. He waits for the moan and then stops moving forward, but around instead. He keeps his cock circling inside Helena and listens as she starts to moan a different moan, a pleasurable now fuck the shit out of me moan. He thrusts in and out, backwards and forwards again. Eduardo is also fucking her backwards and forwards, in and out of her wet pussy with the precision of the Chinese Army. Both cocks are deep inside her, and then both cocks are almost completely outside of her. Helena can only concentrate on the dick in her mouth, the only one she is able to control.

Luigi has his sights on her cunt though. He throws a look at Eduardo that needs no words. Slowly, Eduardo sends his cock into her, and then out. Slowly again, he drives it into her and then withdraws completely as Luigi removes his dick from Helena's mouth. Eduardo removes his condom while Luigi coats his with a little bit of the moisturizer that had facilitated her massage. He's in her cunt like an Italian on spaghetti, his entire Latino self so deep inside her that she has to remind herself of the shift, his dick suddenly feeling larger than she knows it is. Luigi loves drawing a reaction, and when he sees that his full throttle assault has her gasping, he keeps pounding her cunt this way until he is too close to shooting for his own comfort. He lingers momentarily so that the urge dissipates, and then proceeds to fuck the lively pussy in a more contained manner. Besides, Helena's cunt isn't going anywhere anytime soon.

Helena's mouth around his cock is everything Eduardo thought it would be when he watched her work the others. Like her pussy, Helena's mouth is experienced. So experienced in fact that whatever you threw at it, instinct would have her know exactly what to do with it. She sucks on Eduardo's dick with every part of her mouth. Her tongue finds the slit in his head as she lets some of his shaft escape her. Then she circles it and lets her tongue guide her teeth along the meat, mock biting into it as she makes her way remarkably close to the base. She seems to manage a base-jump a few times, Eduardo letting his cock sit in her throat while he takes in the sight and processes the sensation. Helena obviously loves sucking cock.

Luigi brings her to an eclectic orgasm. His thrusting so slow, so deliberately and almost agonizingly slow that the entire orgasm catches her by surprise and for a little while she can't breathe. Luigi continues to fuck her as she makes her way back to begin, trying for what they've watched Eduardo achieve a couple of times. It doesn't work as well and so he simply sends his dick into her for as many thrusts as it takes for him to cum. He keeps his cock inside her post-climax though, and it is her pussy that has him hard and ready to fuck her again within minutes. He withdraws, and re-suits.

Pedro cums shortly after Luigi, the hotness of Helena's ass driving his cock over the edge, having him fuck her as though it were impossible for her to break.

He too keeps his cock inside her after his load is shot and then, only once his dick has gone hard again, does he remove it and replace the condom. They have obviously made the conscious decision to make the absolute best of this day. Helena is herself prepared for whatever they will throw at her, knowing that she will only be seeing the possibility of action after the summer now, when the kids have returned to school. Pedro and Luigi watch as Eduardo's cock dips in and out of Helena's mouth, stroking their cocks for the show.

Eduardo's cock is the focus again, no trace of any jizz yet. He climbs over Helena and finds her cunt with his mouth. Fucking her mouth with his dick, he tackles the depths of her pussy with his tongue. Luigi and Pedro part her legs and lift them so that her vagina is completely in Eduardo's mouth and her ass is slightly off the chaise. Eduardo's dick hardens even more in her mouth now, the man excited by the taste of her in his mouth. He fucks harder and harder into her mouth, his cock moving over her perfect teeth, enjoying it. They both know that his dick is too aggressive for her to handle bringing him to a climax in the current position, so her cunt becomes the next port of call. But not just yet....

Pedro allows Luigi the first entry into

the exposed asshole. Eduardo raises himself slightly so that Luigi can get under her, almost sending his cock into her while kissing the foot in his hand. Pedro kisses the other foot, holding it so that her legs remain parted and she remains lifted without actually having to do anything herself. The mouth on her cunt and the cock in her mouth make everything else in the room background. She has no idea when Luigi exits and Pedro enters, only that her ass feels constantly occupied by dick. Eduardo's cock has the full run of her mouth, and his tongue quickly has her cunt send his cock a cordial invite to a private party.

When Eduardo's massive rod hangs above her pussy, she has already shot off a load into his mouth. Pedro and Luigi have resumed guard duty and hold each of her legs apart, their own loads shot and their naked dicks hanging limp for the moment as Eduardo prepared to take his own cock to the ball. The meat makes a gentle squeeze into the pussy suffering from mild exhaustion. He drops himself onto her and therefore his cock into her. Filling her with himself, Eduardo gives Helena a long look, into her eyes so that she is unable to look away. He kisses her so that she is aware that he is aware of the appreciation he has for the experience she is giving him, and has given him. He thanks her for the memories as he sends his tongue into her mouth and his cock deeper into her cunt.

Eduardo's strokes are long and deep. He enters her, fills her, and then leaves her void before repeating his mission. He takes her cunt on such a rollercoaster ride that she is suddenly very lightheaded. Helena enjoys Eduardo's cock most of all but will not say it. Luigi knows the location of her g-spot, but Eduardo, he doesn't need to. She allows all of the men the courtesy of thinking that they've rocked her world, and they have. But the dick pushing at every angle of her cunt is the one she'll remember most. And his stamina....

For as long as Eduardo is able to keep fucking her, Helena is in a deep euphoria. He cannot bring himself to cum, not for lack of trying. But after an hour of solid fucking, all he has managed is to bring Helena to an incredible orgasm, guide her back to begin, and arouse Pedro and Luigi again. The sight of Eduardo fucking would arouse anybody. He really knows how to work his entire self into every single stroke. With each stroke of his cock, Eduardo is felt in his entirety. This is what Helena enjoys, the completeness of the fuck. In a different world, this man would be the ideal lover. In this one, he's just the thickest cock to have graced her cunt.

Luigi and Pedro drop their cocks into Helena's mouth again, sending Eduardo into a frenzy. He starts to thrust harder and harder, faster and faster, deeper and deeper, needing that tightness, needing it to be his cock being squeezed into her tight hole. He mouths off at Luigi who takes his cock from Helena and slides under Eduardo so that he has access to her cunt and ass with his cock were she to be adjusted slightly. After more direction from Eduardo, the adjustment takes place and Luigi is soon struggling to get his dick into the same hole that has been monopolized by Eduardo's meat. It's a minute or two but eventually he starts to make inroads, slowly edging his way into Helena's cunt alongside Eduardo's massive member. Helena is again laying on Luigi, his cock in her cunt this time though and not her ass.

It's not that Helena has a wide cunt. Eduardo just needs the idea of a squeeze on his meat to motivate him to the edge. It's a fetish of sorts. He loves that he has a supersized cock. And he loves terrorizing small spaces with his enormous dick. This isn't an altogether unacceptable vice. Pedro enjoys Helena's mouth while the two take care of her cunt. Luigi has managed to get all the way inside, but movement is restricted. He allows Eduardo the freedom of the pussy and enjoys the residual friction offered by his cock. The heat inside Helena is the perfect place for both cocks and soon the horizon looms with a fucking fantastic orgasm.

Pedro is the first to shoot a load down Helena's throat. She cums too, giving the needed lubrication for the machines in her pussy to do what they were designed to. There is no escaping the violation now, both cocks having a rather wide range of motion suddenly and both taking full advantage of it. Luigi has needed some sort of control, and now that he has it, his dick wrestles Eduardo's head on and they make a battlefield of Helena's vagina. She rewards them by layering the battlefield in thick oil to keep them mobile.

Luigi shoots first, filling his condom with cum and also pushing against Eduardo's cock as his own dick expands and contracts, pulsating during ejaculation. Eduardo capitalizes on this brief extra squeeze and sends several thrusts not just into Helena but also against Luigi's cock which has been generous enough to stay hard. Eduardo shoots his load and continues to thrust, even as Luigi exits. Pedro watches as Luigi withdraws and joins him, both of them now watching Eduardo fuck Helena with the force of a man who is yet to cum. Everyone knows that he's cum, but Helena isn't complaining.

Eduardo withdraws, removing his condom so quickly as he does that a bit of it is left in her. He pulls it out gently before sending his cock back into her. He pulls a solid triple orgasm from her before sending his cock into her ass in one movement and taking a two dozen-stroke dash to the best orgasm of the day. Everyone else jerks off over the scene and cums on Helena and the chaise. She thanks each cock with a sensual suck as each tongue thanks her cunt with a few licks. Everyone is unable and unwilling to move for two full hours after the final set of orgasms. Nobody speaks; nobody needs to.

After everyone has done their own thing, cleaning up individually, needing to for fear of a rematch, the three thank Helena. She thanks them and makes sure that they've remembered to take the check. Everything inside her wants them to stay the night and keep her company for one last time. But she knows that this isn't Oz and that she needs to get back to her life, and herself. She also knows that there will be other opportunities like this one, later. There is no rush, and no need to overkill it. But Eduardo's cock is tempting, and the other cocks are fucking awesome in their own right. So why not give one more round on the Ferris wheel. Who need know anyway? Mature pussy tells no tales after all.

Eduardo's lips find her cunt first, then Pedro's. Luigi is immediately in her ass. The three fuck her in an intense series of ass and pussy rotations until there are no condoms left and the sun hangs in the sky at three o'clock. Helena knows that she will not be able to stand so she makes no attempt to, watching as they get ready, cleaning up again and getting dressed quickly so as not to indulge their cocks which look like they might stand at any moment. The three leave her on the chaise and head for the fridge, grabbing a cold drink each and a fruit. They look at her, wink and then leave. She falls into a ten-minute sleep and wakes as rested as though she's slept a full night.

The pristine water of her swimming pool covers her completely as she dives into it. Helena disappears under the water for the length of the pool and emerges on the far end without getting out of the water. She thinks of the three Latinos leaving, for the last time. There were no formal goodbyes, the last formality being the check. Her house will be abuzz soon, the cleaning staff arriving tomorrow to prepare the house for the arrival of the children in two days. Helena is grateful that she doesn't need to leave the water to open the gate, Eduardo having been shown the technicalities of how to get them out enough times. She disappears under the water again and swims to the other side of the pool....

AUTHOR'S NOTE

Readers: I want to expand a few of the stories
to see where the characters can be explored
further. If there are any of the stories that you
would like to read more about again, I'd love
to hear from you!

Visit my blog at www.kellenprime.com

Join my newsletter for free exclusive previews
http://www.kellenprime.com/in

Follow me on Twitter at
http://www.twitter.com/kellenprime

Like my page on Facebook at
http://www.facebook.com/kellenprime

Discover my books at major ebook retailers
everywhere.

www.ingramcontent.com/pod-product-compliance
Lightning Source LLC
Chambersburg PA
CBHW022021240626
47154CB00007B/2209